Beat Surrender

Bob Stone

'Follow your heart'

Beaten Track
www.beatentrackpublishing.com

Beat Surrender

First published 2019 by Beaten Track Publishing

ISBN: 978 1 78645 286 3

Cover Design: Trevor Howarth

Beaten Track Publishing,
Burscough, Lancashire.
www.beatentrackpublishing.com

To the memory of my parents,
John and Nancy Stone

Contents

Part One 1
Chapter One 3
Chapter Two 7
Chapter Three 11
Chapter Four 15
Chapter Five 19
Chapter Six 23
Chapter Seven 27
Chapter Eight 29
Chapter Nine 33
Chapter Ten 37
Chapter Eleven 41
Chapter Twelve 45
Chapter Thirteen 51
Chapter Fourteen 55
Chapter Fifteen 59
Chapter Sixteen 63
Chapter Seventeen 67
Chapter Eighteen 71
Chapter Nineteen 77
Chapter Twenty 81
Chapter Twenty-One 85
Chapter Twenty-Two 89
Chapter Twenty-Three 93
Chapter Twenty-Four 97
Chapter Twenty-Five 101
Chapter Twenty-Six 107
Chapter Twenty-Seven 111

Part Two 115
Chapter One 117
Chapter Two 121
Chapter Three 127
Chapter Four 131
Chapter Five 135
Chapter Six 141
Chapter Seven 145
Chapter Eight 149
Chapter Nine 153
Chapter Ten 159
Chapter Eleven 165
Chapter Twelve 169
Chapter Thirteen 173
Chapter Fourteen 181
Chapter Fifteen 189
Chapter Sixteen 193
Chapter Seventeen 199
Chapter Eighteen 203
Chapter Nineteen 207
Chapter Twenty 213
Chapter Twenty-One 219
Chapter Twenty-Two 225
Chapter Twenty-Three 229
Chapter Twenty-Four 233
Chapter Twenty-Five 239
Epilogue 245
Praise For *Missing Beat* ***247***
Acknowledgements 249
About the Author 251
By the Author 252
Beaten Track Publishing 253

PART ONE

Chapter One

JOEY CALE STARED out at the grey River Mersey, watching a huge white liner ease past on the horizon, its movement so imperceptible at that distance it looked like it was standing still. Joey didn't recognise the blue logo on the side, perhaps because he only knew the names of a few liner companies, or perhaps because this one only existed in this world. He didn't know.

There were a great many things Joey didn't know anymore. He'd spent the first seventeen years of his life firmly believing that, no matter what you saw in TV programmes like Doctor Who, there was only one planet Earth, only one universe. Then, for reasons he still didn't fully understand, he had discovered that other versions of Earth did exist, all with their own rules. At least, that had been the case for the world in which he had found himself. Now, he was somewhere else again, and he had no idea where.

He had been standing staring out across the river all morning, trying to get his head together, trying to ignore the pangs of hunger reminding him he hadn't eaten since...when? It was hard to say. The shock of finding someone else living in his parents' house—*his* house—had sent him into a blind panic. Desperately seeking the familiar, he had come to the river to think. But not about Emma. There were some things he just couldn't think about right now.

By his reckoning, it had been about a week since he'd left the familiarity of his house to get his A' Level results. It had been a couple of days at the most since he and his new friend Raj had stood on the beach below, talking to a man—whose name probably wasn't Remick—and learning the truth.

It had been less than twenty-four hours since he'd watched Emma die in front of him.

All Joey had wanted was to go home, go back to something approaching normal life. Now, that seemed further away than ever, and he had nowhere to go, nobody to run to. He didn't know where Raj or Anna and the kids had ended up. They could have landed anywhere. Joey was alone in another strange world with no idea what to do next.

Despite his best efforts, his mind kept taking him back to Emma. He had known her for such a short space of time, yet all they had been through together had forged a bond between them. Whether that bond would have grown into something more, he would never know. He had watched in horror as the demon calling itself Saunders had lashed out at her. He had cradled her dead body in his arms and tried to bring her home. He had felt the void in his heart when she had disappeared. And he had started to grieve over losing her, not once, but twice.

And yet…

It *had* been her. The girl he had bumped into when he backed away from what was no longer his house was definitely Emma. Nobody else looked like that. Admittedly, the Emma he'd known had been living on her own for a while and she looked like it, whereas this girl was somehow neater; her clothes were newer.

But the most significant difference was that she appeared to have no idea who Joey was. When he'd called her name, she'd stared at him in horror, told him he had the wrong person and then hurried away, leaving Joey standing on the street feeling like an idiot. All he knew for sure was that this version of Liverpool clearly had its own Emma Winrush, but she had never known Joey Cale, and he had no place in this world.

So, Joey stood looking out onto a Mersey that wasn't his Mersey under a sky that wasn't his sky. All around him, people were getting on with their lives, walking their dogs or just taking in the air. A large gull landed on the railings nearby and fixed its yellow eyes on him with an unnerving stare. It stayed for a while, but its conversation was minimal, and eventually, once it realised Joey had nothing good to eat about his person, it flapped its wings and flew off.

A noise cut through the swish of the waves and the seagulls' squawks. Tinny music, coming from somewhere nearby. It was a sound Joey hadn't heard for a while, and it took him a second or two to figure out it was coming from his pocket. Somehow, impossibly, his phone, which had remained silent and devoid of signal all the time he had been away, was now ringing.

Chapter Two

JOEY FUMBLED HIS phone out of his pocket and dropped it onto the sand-drift at his feet. He snatched it up again and hit the answer key before it stopped.

"Hello?" he said hesitantly.

There was a burst of static on the other end, and then a male voice spoke. It sounded far away, almost as though it was someone speaking in another room.

"Joey?"

"Who's this?" The voice sounded vaguely familiar from somewhere.

"Don't talk, just listen. You've got to move. You've got to get away from there."

"Why? What—"

"Just do it. Go anywhere. We'll find you, but go *now.* Oh, and Joey? Look out for the Green Jackets."

Before he could ask anything else, the phone went dead. Joey checked the call log, but the screen displayed an *unknown caller* message. *Green Jackets?* He put his phone away and looked around.

Between the beach and the road, there was a grass-covered field. It was a popular destination for dog walkers, and on a warm, sunny morning like this, it was already starting to get busy. A man threw a Frisbee for an enthusiastic border collie while two Jack Russell terriers rolled over each other in a play-fight to reach a ball. But in the distance, Joey spotted them: three men in long, green coats.

Pleasant as the weather was, it hardly called for sunglasses, yet all three wore them, and they had the same hairstyle, slicked back harshly from their foreheads. Two were dark and one was blonde; even from a distance, Joey could tell the blonde was dyed rather than natural, but the hair, the shades and the coats seemed to be some kind of uniform.

The three men climbed onto the field from the car park and walked in a rough triangular formation, one in front, the other two slightly behind. They weren't talking to each other but were quite clearly looking for something. *Or someone.* Joey eased through the railings that bordered the coastal path and dropped down the short distance to the beach below. Keeping close to the wall so he couldn't be seen from the path above, he moved off, not running but moving as quickly as he could, glancing back towards the steps that led down from the path to the beach. When he was sure nobody was watching, he broke into a run.

He ran for maybe five or ten minutes before he felt safe enough to slow down. Behind him, the beach stretched out, but there was no sign of the men in long coats. He stopped for a moment, bent over, his hands on his knees, getting his breath back. Once his breathing and heart rate had slowed to something approaching normal, he started to walk. The car park receded behind him, and to his right the grass was replaced by sand littered with bricks worn smooth by the tide where, according to his father, houses built too close to the river had crumbled and collapsed.

Joey kept going, knowing the beach would take him past Hightown and Formby and all the way to Southport. He was just wondering how far he should go when his phone rang again. He pulled it out of his pocket and answered it immediately.

"Did you get away?" asked the voice on the other end.

"Yes, but—"

"Did you see them? The Green Jackets? Guys in long coats and shades?"

"Yes, there were three of them. But..." Joey stopped. "Look, who *is* this?"

"Where are you now?" the voice wanted to know, ignoring Joey's question altogether.

"On the beach," he began, but stopped again, suddenly suspicious. "Tell me who you are first. You could be anyone. How did you get my number?"

"You don't know me," the caller said. "But we have mutual friends. We'll tell you all you need to know when we find you, but for now, you'll have to trust me."

"Why should I?" Joey demanded.

"Because Raj will kick my arse for me if I lose you. Is that good enough?"

"Raj?" Joey repeated. "He's *here*?" He had an idea. "Has he still got his dog? Did Sheba make it here too?"

"Don't know about any Sheba, but Misha's here. Nice try, though. Now, where are you?"

"Just past the coastal erosion," Joey answered, a little more reassured. "Heading towards Hightown."

"Okay. Hang on."

Joey heard muffled voices in the background, then the caller came back on the line.

"Double back but take the upper path along the side of the golf course. You know the one I mean?"

"Yes, I do."

"Cool. There's a footpath that brings you out by the entrance to the golf club. Wait there. We'll be ten minutes."

The line went dead as the caller hung up.

Joey followed his instructions. He picked his way over the eroded bricks up to the path at the top. Following it, and keeping a lookout for any men in long coats, he passed through what had probably at one time been a narrow gateway. To his left was the entrance sign for the golf club. He stopped there as instructed and waited, with no idea who he was waiting for or how they were coming. Cars went past, but none of them stopped or even slowed. A movement behind startled him, but it was only two crows, fluttering down on inky-black wings to settle on a fence. Joey was briefly reminded of *The Birds*—a film his dad had been watching one night a few years back, in which Joey had become engrossed—but he pushed the thought from his head and concentrated on the road.

True to the caller's word, just over ten minutes after the phone call had ended, Joey heard the sound of an engine slowing and saw a large black people carrier approach. Keeping the path behind him in case he had to turn and run, he waited as the car pulled up alongside him. The tinted front window opened, and Joey saw a face he didn't recognise: a man probably in his fifties with a shaved head and a small beard.

"Jump in the back, Joey," he said.

Joey hesitated.

"Come on," the man urged. "It won't take the Green Jackets long to suss out which way you went."

Joey hurried over and slid open the car's rear door. As he climbed inside, he discovered he was not alone in the back.

"About time!" Raj said with a grin. "What kept you?"

Chapter Three

RAJ!" JOEY SHOOK his friend's hand. "Thank God you're okay! When did you get here?"

"Six months ago," Raj said. When he saw Joey's confusion, he added, "It's a long story. I'll tell you as we go."

"Six months? Where have you been?"

"All in good time," Raj replied and then said to the driver, "We need to move, Geoff."

Geoff nodded and eased the car into gear. As it moved off, Raj leaned back in his seat and seemed to relax a little. "I suppose this is all a bit weird for you," he said to Joey.

"Yes, it is. I mean, six months? How? You went through that portal thing yesterday."

"For you, maybe. Not for me."

"What about Anna? Did she make it? And the kids? Ruby and Evan?"

"The kids are fine," Raj assured him. "You'll see. Anna—well, that's a bit more complicated. I'll tell you everything in a bit."

Joey sat in silence for a while, taking it in. He toyed with mentioning Emma but decided against it for now. His thoughts were interrupted by Geoff calling out from the front seat.

"Level crossing's down."

Joey had a flashback to the last time he had seen this particular level crossing. There had been a train paused right across it, going nowhere, and he, Raj and Misha the dog had jumped over the barriers. But it wasn't *this* level crossing. It was another one in another world, even though Joey could still feel the ache in his wrist from his bad landing.

"Try and do a U," Raj advised. He reached down onto the floor of the car and picked up a new rucksack. "This is for you," he told Joey. "There's stuff you might need. I don't imagine you have any money for a start. Not the right money, anyway."

Before Joey could ask what the right money might be, Geoff swore loudly. Joey looked out of the car window; they were side-on to the crossing gates, and a white van was heading rapidly towards them.

"Move it!" Raj shouted. "Come on, Geoff!"

Geoff tried to slam the car into reverse but stalled instead and swore again.

"Joey, get out and go," Raj said. "Go over the bridge. We'll hold them off."

"But who—"

"Don't ask. Just go!"

Joey grabbed the rucksack and opened the door, fumbling with the handle. The white van was almost on them as Joey took off for the railway bridge. As he neared the top, he heard the impact of the van hitting Raj's car and shunting it into the crossing barrier. He peered over the side of the bridge and saw the van doors open, a flash of green coats as men climbed out. Then he ran across the bridge and down the stairs, leaping two at a time.

He reached the bottom and looked back, nearly jumping out of his skin when a horn sounded, followed by a roar as a train pulled into the station next to the crossing. On an impulse, Joey raced onto the platform and boarded the train, pushing his way through the bewildered passengers trying to get off. He found a seat and sat low in it, pulling up his coat collar as he watched anxiously out of the window, desperate for the train to depart.

A man in a long green coat charged along the platform, knocking people out of his way to make the train. He got close enough for Joey to see his face. The man was younger than Joey had first thought, his forehead peppered with acne. Despite the hair and the sunglasses, there was something vaguely familiar about the face, but Joey couldn't put his finger on what it was.

The man almost reached the open carriage door, but he was too late. The doors slid shut, and the train moved off without him. Joey relaxed slightly once the train began to move. Now all he had to do was decide where to get off and what to do next.

Chapter Four

Emma Winrush put the face she saw in the mirror down to the fact that she was still shaken up from her encounter. After all, her hands had been trembling as she'd poured the uneaten cornflakes into the bin. It was all so weird. If she hadn't gone to the corner shop to buy the milk for her cereal in the first place, she would not have bumped into the boy, the strange, intense boy, who knew her name even though she had never seen him before in her life.

And yet...

Emma didn't know him. She *knew* she didn't know him, but there was something about his face that nagged at the back of her mind. It was that feeling, along with the fact he clearly knew her, which disturbed her. Had to be.

She'd washed her cereal bowl and come upstairs to clean her teeth, watching her reflection in the mirror above the sink as she did so. Her purple hair was tied back in a loose ponytail. Her black eyeliner was toned down as it always was for school these days—ever since Mrs. Bowes put her on report for it. Her face was pale, but no paler than normal. Then suddenly, and just for a second, she thought she caught a glimpse of a different Emma. Same purple hair, though not tied back, no eyeliner, and even though there was no sound, the face seemed to be shouting.

Then it was gone; Emma's familiar face looked back at her. She shook her head. She must have been more tired than she'd thought, but one thing was for sure. If she ever saw that boy again, she would probably kill him.

She hadn't slept much last night, which didn't help matters. Her mum had stayed up after Emma had turned in, but Emma always remained awake and alert, ever since the night her mum had fallen out of her armchair and pulled it down on top of her. She hadn't been hurt, but Emma had to come down and lift the chair off her. Now, whenever her mum stayed up—drinking—Emma couldn't sleep until she'd heard her stumble up the stairs. Last night, it had been nearly half past two, according to the alarm clock she kept by her bed. No wonder she was tired.

As she washed her hands, she was faced with another mystery. On the side of her wrist, there was a scar she'd never noticed before. She often found bruises she didn't remember acquiring, but very rarely a cut, and this was an old one too, long healed. She shook her head. Too much on her mind.

Emma went downstairs and picked up her school bag, which she'd packed the night before, as she always did. On the increasingly rare occasions when her mum got up before school, Emma liked to be ready to go as quickly as she could, but after last night's late session, there was no chance of that today. Emma pulled on her coat, grabbed her keys and phone and left the house. Time was, her mum and dad would both have called goodbye to her and told her to have a good day. But no more. Her dad was out of the area; her mum was just out of it.

Emma looked around cautiously as she left the house. No sign of any strange boy loitering, she breathed a sigh of relief and went to catch her bus to school. It wasn't that she was in any hurry to get there; she hated the place and all the fake idiots in her class, but it was somewhere to go that wasn't home—until she left at the end of the year, at least. There was even a possibility she might still pass some of her exams and make something of herself. She wouldn't be going to uni, she knew that. There wasn't much money coming in since her dad had left, and anyway, she knew if she left too, it would destroy her mum. But at least with some exams behind her she might have a better chance of finding a job, not like some of the other wasters of her age, who had left after their GCSEs and now just hung around the shopping area in Crosby, doing nothing, going nowhere.

The bus arrived as Emma reached the bus stop; she showed her pass to the driver and found a seat near the front. Behind her, she could hear the over-loud conversations of the other kids talking about last night's telly or who they claimed to have snogged. None of it interested Emma. She put her earphones in and found a decent tune to listen to on her phone to blot out the noise.

The morning passed by without incident, and it was only after lunch—spent on her own in a corner of the canteen as usual—that the day started to get stranger. She had just taken her seat in Mr. Mayhew's English class when the door opened and Miss Evans, the headteacher's secretary, came in. She took Mr. Mayhew to one side, had a quick word and then left.

"Emma," Mr. Mayhew said, a concerned look on his face, "Mr. Burrows would like you to go to his office, please."

A buzz ran around the room, and a hot rush of embarrassment flooded Emma's face as she felt the eyes of everyone in the class on her. Chantelle Drayton went, "Wooo!" and someone else laughed.

"Why, Sir?" Emma asked. "Do you know?"

"No, I don't. Emma. He didn't say. I wouldn't keep him waiting, though. Come on, now."

Emma got to her feet and, glancing back at Mr. Mayhew, who was watching her go, hurried from the room.

As she rushed along the corridors to Mr. Burrows' office, Emma's head whirled. She knew she wasn't in trouble. She kept her head down and tried not to be noticed most of the time. Was it her mum? Had she finally done something *really* stupid?

When she reached the office, Miss Evans, who always reminded Emma of a slightly nervous bird, was waiting outside.

"I'll just let him know you're here," she told Emma and knocked on the office door. Mr. Burrows called for her to come in, and as the door opened, Emma froze in horror. Sitting in a chair opposite Mr. Burrows, his legs stretched out as if he owned the place, was a Green Jacket. Panic rose in Emma's chest as the door closed, obscuring her view. What did the Green Jackets want with her? She hadn't done anything wrong. But she'd heard all the stories. If the GJs came for you, they came for you and that was that.

Before the door could open again, she was running down the corridor towards the school entrance. She slapped the door release button and flew from the building, down the drive and out of the school gates.

Once on the street, she paused briefly, glancing nervously behind her to make sure she wasn't being followed, then had to make a quick decision as to which way to go next. One way led to the town centre, where she might be able to lose herself amongst shoppers, or hide in a café. The other led down a long road to the station. She took the latter option and started to run.

By the time she reached the station, she was out of breath but in luck because a train to Southport was pulling in. She flashed her travel pass at the ticket inspector and ran onto the platform. There, she nearly stopped dead. A Green Jacket was on the platform, shoving his way through passengers and trying to get to the train. *He can't be after me. There hasn't been time*!

Keeping her head down, she boarded the train a carriage away from the one the GJ was trying to reach, and was relieved when the doors closed and the train moved off, leaving the Green Jacket stranded on the platform.

Emma settled back in her seat, her mind racing. She couldn't understand why the Green Jackets were after her. They were only interested in serious criminals, terrorists and anarchists, or so they said, and Emma was certainly none of those. As she wrestled with that, and with the small matter of where she was going to go next, she got her next shock. Through the window in the door which separated the carriages, she could see, slumped in a seat and looking anxiously out of the window, the unmistakable figure of the strange boy who had startled her in the street.

Chapter Five

EMMA FELT A surge of anger. On top of everything else that had happened so far that day—and it was still only early afternoon—this boy seemed to be stalking her. Was he something to do with the Green Jackets? Had he been planted on this train to intercept her? Two things persuaded her otherwise. The first was that she doubted anyone could have predicted she would run from the school and get on this train when she did. The second was that the boy didn't seem to have noticed her. More than that, he didn't seem to be looking, or even aware of his surroundings. He was just staring out of the window, and he looked tired, as if he might doze off at any moment. If Emma got off the train at the next stop or the one after, he probably wouldn't notice at all.

Her thoughts were interrupted by a chime from her bag. She reached in and took out her mobile: a new text message, from the school.

> Emma Winrush is to return to the school immediately. Failure to do so will result in disciplinary action.
>
> Please reply to this message.

Emma stared at the words a second longer and then deleted the message. She was tempted to open one of her social media accounts. Lifeplace was bound to be buzzing with speculation from her classmates about where she'd gone, but she really didn't want to see their smug, stupid comments. She had to decide what to do, and quickly. Other people would have friends or family they could run to, people who would offer them help or support. Emma had nobody. Her mum would freak, and her dad, loved up as he was with his new wife, would probably put her in the car and bring her straight back.

Emma looked again at the boy in the next carriage. She still couldn't put her finger on why he seemed familiar. He was around her age but definitely didn't go to her school. He probably lived locally and was one of those faces you just saw around the place but didn't really register. So how did he know her? Despite a nagging feeling that it might not be a good idea, she suddenly had a burning curiosity to find out. She stood up and walked unsteadily along the moving train into the next carriage.

His face when he realised she was sitting opposite him was priceless. He looked for all the world like he had been slapped hard and didn't know why.

"Hi." Emma sounded more confident than she felt. "I saw you from the next carriage. You want to tell me what that was all about this morning?"

He clearly had no idea what to say. Emma could see he was thinking, and that the next thing to come out of his mouth might not be the truth.

"Sorry," he said. "You just look like someone I know."

"Someone called Emma? Someone with the same name as me?"

"Yes," he said slowly. "What are the odds?"

"Crap. Do you want me to ask again, or do you need a bit more time to think of an answer? Because that one was pathetic."

He stared at her, and Emma saw pain flash across his face.

"You wouldn't believe me," he said.

"I don't believe you now. So try me."

He paused, rubbing a hand across his forehead as if he had a headache.

"Okay," he said. "I knew someone called Emma who looked a lot like you. She—something happened to her. Sorry. I didn't mean to scare you."

"What happened to her?"

"It doesn't matter. Look, I'm getting off in a minute. I won't bother you again." He sat back in his seat, the conversation apparently closed.

Emma stared out of the window to get her bearings and caught sight of her reflection in the glass. Only it wasn't her reflection. It was that other Emma, the one she had seen in the bathroom mirror, the one who looked tired and somehow older. The one who was silently shouting. For no apparent reason, the scar on her wrist began to itch, and she rubbed at it.

The boy opposite her noticed and sat upright. "What happened to it?"

"I don't know."

"Did you do it yourself?"

"What? No!" Emma was horrified. "Why?"

"We need to get off this train. Next stop." He stood up. "Come on."

Emma sat tight. "No way. I'm not going anywhere with you until you tell me—"

"No time," he replied firmly. The train was slowing down into the next station. "Come on. *Now.*"

Emma had no idea why she did it, but she stood and followed him to the door of the train. The train pulled into the station, and Emma spotted the station name: Freshfield. They had come further than she thought. When the train stopped and the doors opened, the boy grabbed her hand and pulled her out onto the platform. That was enough for Emma. She snatched her hand back and refused to move.

"That's it! I don't know who you are, or what's going on, but—"

"I'm Joey Cale," he said. "You *are* Emma Winrush, aren't you?"

"Yes I am, but—"

"Then I might have put you in danger. We need to get moving."

Emma followed him out of the station, waving her travel pass at the ticket inspector, who shouted after Joey. Joey, however, was not listening. He rushed out onto a quiet, tree-lined street and looked in both directions.

"This way," he said, nodding to the left.

"No." Emma stayed put. "Not until you tell me what's going on."

"I will, but not here. Is your arm still itching?"

"Yes," she said, suddenly more aware of it than ever.

"Then it isn't safe. We need to lose ourselves."

"What's my arm got to do with it? Just what the hell is this all about?"

"It's a warning. Or it was. I don't know the rules here. We can't risk it. We need to get somewhere safe, and I know just the place."

Chapter Six

EMMA HAD BEEN to the Freshfield Nature Reserve many times when she was younger. Her parents used to take her, and they'd spent many happy hours wandering through the acres of pine woods, throwing monkey nuts to the red squirrels, some of whom were tame enough to take nuts right out of Emma's eager hands. She hadn't been there for years, but the place had hardly changed, apart from a brightly painted snack stand near the entrance; Joey spotted it too.

"I need something to eat," he said. "You hungry?"

"I haven't got any money."

"I have, I think."

Joey took off the rucksack which had been slung over his shoulder and ran his hand over the side pockets. He unzipped one and fished out a wallet, which looked to Emma to be brand-new. It also seemed to be stuffed with notes—something else to ask him about. Joey took out one of the notes and studied it, his expression suggesting he'd never seen one before.

"They *are* different," he said, surprising Emma with a laugh. He went over to the stand and ordered a sandwich and a coffee. "Do you want anything?" he called back.

"Just a coffee," she said.

Joey ordered it, and when the man on the stand told him the price, he stepped back, visibly shocked. "How much? That's a rip-off!"

"Do you want it or not?" the man asked.

Joey didn't reply, just peeled a couple of notes off the bundle in his wallet and handed them over.

"Everything's expensive these days," Emma reasoned. "Or hadn't you noticed?"

"I've been away," he said evasively. "If you want a cigarette, it's probably best to have one now before we go into the woods."

Emma frowned. "I don't smoke. Why did you say that?"

"Oh, er… No reason."

"Did *she* smoke? This other Emma of yours?"

Joey didn't reply. He took the coffees and the sandwich which the man on the snack stand had slapped on the counter and handed Emma her drink.

"Come on," he said. "We need to get into the woods."

Emma was struck, once again, by how bizarrely this day was turning out. It had been less than an hour since she had run from school, and now she was going into the pine woods with some weird boy for God knew what reason. She took a sip of her coffee and followed.

The car park was mostly full. There were people with dogs heading down to the beach beyond the pine woods, families with excited children buying bags of monkey nuts at a kiosk. As they walked, Emma noticed Joey eyeing them all with suspicion. What threat did he think an old man with an ageing Labrador could possibly be? What had happened to him? And, more importantly, what did he mean by *I might have put you in danger*? But there was something about him Emma couldn't put her finger on. Something honest, something that made her trust him. The danger wasn't coming from him; it was coming from somewhere else, and that was what worried her.

Joey chose, seemingly at random, one of the many paths into the woods and started down it. "There aren't as many people," he explained.

"Isn't it better if there *are* other people around?" Emma asked. "If there's someone after you, isn't it safer with *lots* of people? No-one's going to do anything with witnesses."

"I don't know any of these people," Joey said. "I don't know who to trust. We need a bit of time to figure out what's going on."

They carried on down the path, further into the woods. The patches of sunlight shining down through the trees became sparser and the air was noticeably cooler. The scent of pine was everywhere, and every so often Emma heard a scuffling amongst the branches which she really hoped was squirrels. She had always loved this place, but now the noises were making her jumpy, and she didn't like it. This was ridiculous.

"Stop a minute," she said. Joey didn't seem to have heard, so she repeated. "Joey, *stop.*"

He stopped walking and turned to face her.

"I'm not going any further until you tell me what's going on."

Joey sighed and looked around. "This is as good a place as any. Let's sit for a bit."

He sat and leaned back against a tree. Emma came to join him, feeling the bed of compacted pine needles in case it was damp. It felt springy, but dry, so she sat too.

Joey calmly unwrapped his sandwich and took a large bite. "This," he said as he chewed, "is definitely not worth the money." Emma stared at him. He looked up from his sandwich and caught her gaze. "Drink your coffee before it gets cold."

Emma did as he suggested. The coffee was hot and strong, and she felt better for drinking it. "Okay, Joey Cale. Talk to me."

Joey took a long slow breath. "I'm not from this world," he said. "I'm from another version of Earth which had another version of you—another Emma Winrush. We became friends, I suppose, and I watched her die."

Emma could tell from his troubled face that he was telling the truth, and it was like someone had pulled a rug out from under her feet. What he had just told her was impossible, and yet he clearly believed every word.

"Go on," she said. And Joey did.

Chapter Seven

GEOFF TRAYNOR HAD braced for the impact, but when the van hit their car, he was still thrown sideways, the seat belt digging painfully into his shoulder.

"You okay?" he called to Raj in the back.

"Fine," Raj answered through gritted teeth. "Did he get away?"

"Looks like," Geoff said. He looked through the side window, now spiderwebbed with cracks. The kid had legged it onto the station, but one of the Green Jackets had followed. Two more of them were climbing out of the van. "You need to get out of here. I'll keep them busy."

Geoff had to force the car door open; it had buckled on impact. He stood facing the two Green Jackets.

"What the hell was that about?" he asked them. "You could have killed me!"

"Where's the boy gone?" one of the Green Jackets demanded.

"I don't know what you mean."

"Don't play stupid. That lad who just got out of your car. Where's he gone?"

"Oh, him?" Geoff played innocent. "He was just some kid who wanted a lift. Why? What's he done?"

The other Green Jacket had produced a tablet computer from his pocket and was looking at the screen.

"Geoffrey Traynor," he said. "Ex-army. Saw action in Iraq and Afghanistan."

"That's me," Geoff said, trying to lead the Green Jackets away from the car. Raj had managed to get down and out of sight. "What about it? Is there a problem?"

"You just gave that lad a lift? Is that all? Where from?"

"Met him down the beach and we got talking. He asked for a lift to the station, and as I was heading this way..."

Geoff glanced around and saw a number of people had emerged from the station, drawn by the crash, and were gathering in groups, some on their phones, some just watching, but all holding back because of the Green Jackets. It was time to ramp things up a bit.

"Look at the state of my car!" he said loudly. "Who's going to pay for that? I haven't done anything wrong!" He started to move away, getting his phone out. "I need to call the rescue people."

"Put the phone away," the first Green Jacket said, following him. The other Green Jacket stayed where he was. "Now."

"But my car! I can't just leave it here."

"Your vehicle will be taken care of. You're coming with us."

"What for?" Geoff shouted, feigning indignant anger. "I haven't done anything!"

"Geoffrey Traynor," the Green Jacket took a set of handcuffs out of his pocket, "I am lawfully entitled to detain you under the Prevention of Terrorism Act."

"Terrorism?" Geoff protested. "This is victimisation!" He tried to move further away, but the Green Jacket grabbed his arm. *That's more like it.* "Get off me! You can't do this!" He struggled violently—more violently than the Green Jacket's grip warranted—which prompted the second Green Jacket to come over and seize Geoff's other arm. Geoff used all his strength to try to get free, but between them, they managed to drag him behind the van, where they forced him to his knees on the road.

Geoff continued to struggle, shouting "Get off me!" at the top of his voice. From where he and the Green Jackets were, the car was no longer visible, and he hoped Raj would take the opportunity to get away. He was still struggling and yelling when the first punches and kicks landed.

Chapter Eight

EMMA SAT IN silence and listened to Joey's story. She didn't interrupt as he told her about finding himself in a world without people. She kept quiet as he explained how he'd met a girl called Emma Winrush who had gone missing in his own world, and how he and this girl had tried to escape from the world they had found themselves in. She listened in silence as he talked about a man called Remick and another man called Saunders, who were not really men at all, and she heard all about Joey's friends Raj and Anna, and the two children, and how they all seemed to have strange new powers—healing, invisibility, warning against danger.

She didn't even react when Joey told her he had opened a portal between worlds with a beam of light from his heart. But when he told her Emma Winrush had sacrificed her life to save them all, the world fell away beneath her. She wasn't that Emma. She wasn't a hero. She was afraid of wasps and heights and would cross the road to avoid a cat because she didn't like how they looked at her. She was just an ordinary girl and suddenly that didn't feel as though it was enough.

"Oh God," she said finally. "Poor Emma."

"I think she was the strongest of all of us." Joey's eyes glistened with tears. "I tried to bring her home but I ended up here instead. I don't know where she went."

For a moment, there was absolute silence. Even the squirrels had stopped moving around in the trees.

"Who are those guys in green coats?" Joey asked. "I think they are after me."

"The GJs?" Emma asked. "You mean you don't know?"

"Didn't have them where I'm from."

"Lucky you. They're the special police. Anti-Terrorism. They were set up after the bombing."

"What bombing?"

"The bombing of Nelson's Column. Don't tell me you didn't know."

"Didn't happen in my world. Someone blew up Nelson's Column? My God."

"In the middle of summer, when Trafalgar Square was full of tourists. Killed dozens of people when it fell. One of the worst terrorist attacks this country has seen. They reckon the terrorists were after the Houses of Parliament next but blew themselves up instead."

"Who was it?" Joey asked. "ISIS?"

"I don't know who that is," Emma said. "The Government said they were anarchists and set the Green Jackets up in response." She paused. "You really don't know any of this, do you?"

"No. Looks like I've got a lot to learn."

"If the GJs are after you, then you really *are* in trouble. They can do anything they want. There are stories of them beating people up for nothing. And worse. I think they might be after me too. That's why I was on the train. One showed up at my school."

"Why would they be after you? You don't look much like an anarchist to me."

Emma found herself smiling against her will. "Neither do you," she said. "So what are we going to do?"

"I need to get hold of Raj. He seems to know what's going on."

"Raj? Isn't he…?"

"Yes. He's made it here too. Seems he arrived six months ago—don't ask." Joey opened the rucksack again and pulled out the contents, laying them on the ground. There were a couple of packets of sandwiches and a flask of what turned out to be coffee.

"Should have checked first," Emma remarked. "Would have saved you some money."

"It's okay. It's not my money." A fold-up waterproof jacket, a torch and a multi-bladed pocket knife joined the food on the ground before Joey found what he had been looking for; at the bottom of the rucksack was a mobile phone.

"Thought so." He pressed the on switch.

"Don't they have them where you're from?" Emma asked with a half smile.

"They're everywhere," Joey said. "But I wondered if he might have supplied me with one that can't be traced." He frowned as the home screen appeared on the phone. "Pay as you go. Hope there's some credit on it. But Amstrad, though? Really?"

"They're about the biggest," Emma said. "They've bought everyone else out."

Joey checked the address book on the phone and laughed, showing it to Emma. "Misha—that's got to be Raj's number. Unless dogs have phones over here." He tapped the screen to dial the number, switching it to speaker. On the other end, the phone rang and rang and then an automated voice invited Joey to leave a message.

"Hope you're okay," he said. "Give me a call when you get this." He hung up.

He packed everything back into the rucksack, apart from the phone, which he put in his jacket pocket.

"Now we wait, I suppose."

"Wait for what?" Emma asked.

"Wait for Raj to call me back, or for someone to find us."

Chapter Nine

JOEY WOULD LOOK back later and remember that the descent into nightmare started in a slightly farcical way—with a squirrel.

He had been sitting with Emma, waiting and just chatting. He had been trying gently to probe, to find out how she was similar to or different from the Emma he had known, rapidly discovering that one way she was definitely similar was how guarded she was and reluctant to talk about herself. Their rather frustrating conversation was interrupted by a rustle and a soft thump as a red squirrel landed on the ground just a few metres away from them.

"*Look*!" Emma whispered, clearly delighted.

The squirrel sat up like a miniature kangaroo and regarded them.

"He's looking at us!" She beamed, her voice still hushed.

"He's after food," Joey replied.

"I wish I had some nuts."

"It's not something you usually take with you when you're on the run."

Emma looked around and found a couple of monkey nuts which must've been thrown by another visitor to the woods and not yet discovered by the furry population. She knelt down, leaning forward, holding one of the nuts out to the squirrel. "Here you go. Look what I've got for you."

"Careful," Joey cautioned. "They can bite."

"Oh, come on. It's a squirrel! It's gorgeous."

The squirrel continued to eye Emma with suspicion for a minute then slowly edged towards her. Emma glanced at Joey, grinning, taking her eye off the squirrel. Then she shrieked as the squirrel sank its sharp teeth not into the nut, but into the soft flesh of her hand.

"Ow!" she screamed. "Get it off!"

It was perhaps inevitable that it was at this moment Joey's phone began to ring. He fumbled in his pocket with one hand, while trying to bat the squirrel away from Emma with the other. In the end, he dropped his phone and landed a solid slap on the squirrel, which released its grip on Emma's hand and shot back into the trees. Joey grabbed his phone and answered it before it stopped ringing.

"You took your time," Raj said in his ear. "Where are you?"

"Formby pine woods being attacked by a psycho squirrel."

"A… Never mind. Okay. Sit tight. Someone will come and get you. Are you alone?"

"No. I've got Emma Winrush with me."

He glanced over at Emma, who was nursing her hand, pain creasing her face.

"Hmm," Raj said. "You do know it's not the same Emma, don't you?"

"Yes, I know that," Joey replied, sounding rather snappier than he'd intended. "You might want to bring some plasters or something. She's been bitten."

"I'll try," Raj said. "Stay hidden. Stay away from any other people. I'll explain when I see you."

With that, he hung up. Joey put his phone in his pocket and turned his attention to Emma. Blood trickled from the bite on her hand, and she was clearly in a great deal of pain.

"I did warn you," he said, trying to make light of it.

"Hurts," was all Emma could say.

"Let's have a look." He took her hand in his and examined the bite. It was small but nasty.

"It's quite deep," he said. "Have you got a tissue or anything?"

"Don't think so."

Joey felt in his pockets, but he had nothing either. Then he had an idea. "Take your tie off."

"My…oh! I'd forgotten I was wearing it." One-handed, she pulled off her school tie and handed it to Joey. He took the knife out of his rucksack and cut a piece off the tie, which he tied around Emma's hand, covering the bite as best he could.

"It's not exactly sterile," he said, "but it's better than nothing. Hopefully, Raj will bring something with him. Are you okay?"

Emma nodded. "Just a bit shocked, I think. What made it do that?"

"God knows…" Joey began but stopped when he heard, somewhere nearby, a loud snap as someone stepped on a branch. He held his finger to his lips and then helped Emma to her feet. They both stood very still, listening. There was another snap, closer this time. Someone was coming, and they were trying not to be heard.

Joey looked around for the best escape route. Not far away to their left there was a dip in the ground. The top was barely visible through a shroud of bracken. Silently, he pointed, and he and Emma crept as quietly as they could towards it. As they did, he dared a glance back. There was definitely someone there, heading in their direction.

He took Emma's good hand, and they stepped down into the dip, which proved to be deeper than he'd first thought. He sat with his back tight against the wall of soil and bracken roots and Emma did the same. Neither of them dared even to breathe, listening to the soft tread of someone creeping ever closer and then stopping directly above them. Joey craned his neck in an attempt to see who was there and was rewarded with a trickle of sandy soil in his face. He couldn't move to brush it off and had to leave it there, hoping it wouldn't get into his mouth or nose.

Whoever was standing above them stayed there for what seemed like an eternity. Then, as abruptly as they had appeared, the footsteps moved off again. Joey waited for them to become distant before he leaned forward and looked up.

"They've gone," he whispered.

"Who was it?" Emma asked, her voice barely audible.

"No idea." Joey stood up. "We can't stay here, though."

He brushed the soil off his face and clothes while Emma also got up, a movement made awkward by only being able to use one hand. She too dusted herself down.

"Which way?" she asked.

Joey didn't have a chance to decide which direction they should take. A figure stepped out from behind a large pine tree at the top of the rise—a figure in a green coat with slicked-back hair.

"Stay where you are," he said. "You're not going anywhere."

Chapter Ten

RAJEEV CHOWDHURY HAD never really been one for running but he was getting used to it. At school, sports had never interested him. His parents, his father in particular, had encouraged him to believe studying was the only way to achieve anything. If there was time for other things, then fine, but studying always came first. So Raj had studied, succeeded at school and without hesitation went off to study some more, this time with the clear goal of a career in medicine. He didn't expect to end up hiding from the law and being hunted as a terrorist.

Everything had changed the day he found himself in a strange, empty version of the world he knew, and after he met a young man called Joey Cale, Raj's life became more and more surreal, leading to where he was now: crouching behind a wheelie bin in a suburb of Liverpool waiting for a lift to get him to safety.

This is where the years of studying get you. All that work and you end up hiding amongst foul-smelling old takeaway wrappers hoping a friendly face finds you before a very unfriendly one does.

He checked his phone. There was a missed call and a voicemail from the phone he'd given Joey, but it would have to wait, because there was very little charge left and Raj might need it for emergencies. He couldn't afford to worry about Joey right now; if he was in trouble, Raj could do nothing until he was safe himself. Similarly, he couldn't think too much about Geoff, who could be hurt or even dead.

Raj barely recognised himself these days. One of the worst criticisms levelled against him by his mentor at the hospital was that he became too emotionally involved with his patients, which left him open to the stress and depression that plagued many in the profession. But somewhere along the line, he'd become harder, more able to disconnect his emotions. He had a good idea when it happened, too. It was almost certainly the day he witnessed his own death.

That moment had come only a matter of weeks after he'd been separated from Joey on Pendle Hill and ended up in a world he recognised but rapidly discovered he was not where he thought he was.

***

The UK was in a state of crisis, according to the papers he picked up. There had been some sort of disaster in London, and the whole country was on high alert. There were police everywhere.

Trying to find some familiar ground, Raj had headed for the Royal Liverpool Hospital, only to be wrong-footed once more when he watched what seemed to be his mirror image emerge from the building. Confused but fascinated, he had followed this other Raj at a discreet distance. As he did so, he studied his other self. The last time he'd seen a mirror, a rough-looking, unshaven face had stared back at him; a face with bags under the eyes and hair which badly needed a cut. The Raj he was following looked the way he should: tidy and groomed. He was dressed just as Raj always remembered dressing after a shift: in a clean, pressed sweatshirt and comfortable jeans, all topped off with his favourite long, grey woollen coat. This other Raj walked confidently, though there was a tiredness in his tread that betrayed the end of a long shift. Raj remembered being this other person. He remembered how it felt, the exhaustion of having worked long but well, of being able to go home to sleep knowing he had made a difference.

Raj continued to follow his doppelganger down through the city streets to Liverpool Central station, where he would board a train to the other side of the Mersey and the flat he loved going home to in Birkenhead. As he traced the familiar route, Raj had that old feeling of looking forward to going home to bed after a shift. The bed had cost him a lot of money but was worth every penny, and he'd always slept well in it—a deep, often dreamless sleep he hadn't found the likes of since he was ripped away from his home.

At the station, Raj watched his double head for the ticket barrier and realised he would not be able to follow any further; he had no ticket and no money to buy one. He was resigned to watching the other Raj vanish through the barrier and out of his life. But then the other Raj froze, apparently having spotted something on the other side of the barrier. Raj wasn't sure what; all he could see was some blonde man in a long green coat heading toward the ticket barrier from the other side.

Raj's double started to back away from the barrier as the blonde man reached into his pocket and pulled out a leather-bound ID card, waving it in the air. Other passengers heading for the trains scattered, trying to get as far away from the guy as they could. He reached inside his coat again, and Raj was horrified to see him pull out a handgun, which he pointed at the other Raj. As he did so, he shouted, "Rajeev Chowdhury, I have a warrant for your arrest under the Prevention of Terrorism Act. Stop where you are!"

The Raj who belonged in this world hesitated for a moment, torn between flight and surrender, then made his decision and ran. The man in the green coat shouted one more warning, then fired. Raj watched in disbelief as the other Raj's head exploded in a cloud of red and, before his other self's body hit the ground, turned and fled from the station, barging his way through the crowd of passengers who were trying to do the same. He paused outside the station and gritted his teeth, waiting for the unpleasant sensation he had not felt since arriving in this world. The next thing he knew, he was several streets away, vomiting against a graffiti-covered wall. He was safe for now, but he couldn't rest long. He would have to keep moving in case he was recognised.

He kept moving for three days, on foot mainly, trying to limit the use of his unpredictable ability until, quite by chance, the Catesby Foundation saved him.

***

Now, he was hiding behind a wheelie bin, hoping the Catesbys would pick up the tracker on his phone and find him before the Green Jackets did. He could probably teleport away, but there was no guarantee where he'd end up, so it was safer to stay put. It had been one thing teleporting in a world with few people around, but this world was too densely populated to risk it too often. He didn't know what would happen if he landed in a place occupied by another person; it really didn't bear thinking about. Nobody understood how his powers worked, and until they did, they were for emergency use only.

He wondered again if Geoff had managed to get away or if he had lost another friend. Geoff was one of the best, loyal as anyone and full of good humour that kept Raj going through many a bad situation. He also had two young sons and a kind, patient wife, and Raj really didn't relish being the one to have to break the news.

He also wondered about Joey. His arrival was so overdue it had briefly caught everyone by surprise—ironic really, considering they had been waiting for it for so long. The fact Joey had apparently met up with the Emma Winrush of this world was also unexpected; Raj had thought she was being monitored a bit more carefully than that. It was a complication, but the Foundation had overcome much more significant hurdles. If the situation became too complicated, it could be dealt with.

Raj heard a quiet *ping* from his mobile and glanced at the text message that had appeared. *Six minutes*, it said. He just had to stay alive another six minutes and then he could get to the Foundation, maybe have a shower and a change of clothes and then try to find Joey. He just hoped his friend would manage to stay out of trouble long enough.

Chapter Eleven

JOEY HARDLY DARED breathe. He was aware of Emma, motionless, next to him and the man in the green coat staring at them, his gaze flitting from one to the other. Joey couldn't be sure, but he thought it was one of the Green Jackets from the beach—the one with the acne who had seemed familiar.

"You need to come with me. You are to be questioned under the Prevention of Terrorism Act." It sounded unnatural in the Green Jacket's strong Liverpudlian accent, like a well-rehearsed script.

"What have we done?" Joey asked, his mouth dry. "We were just out for a walk in the woods and—"

"Not you," the Green Jacket answered. "Her."

"I haven't done anything!" Emma protested. "I don't know anything."

"You *are* Emma Louise Winrush? Date of birth fifteenth August 2000?"

"Yes, but—"

"Then you're coming with me."

"She hasn't done anything wrong," Joey said. "You've got no right to—"

"See that?" The Green Jacket held up his ID card. "*That's* my right." He let his coat slip open, revealing a shoulder-holstered handgun. "And so's that."

"You don't want her anyway." Joey stepped closer to the Green Jacket, getting between him and Emma. "It's me you're after."

"Is your name Emma Louise Winrush?"

"No, but—"

"Then it's not you I'm here for. I suggest you stand aside, sir, or I will take action against you."

***

Emma watched in horror as Joey fronted up to the Green Jacket. He was trying to buy her time to get away, but she couldn't convince her legs to move. Joey took another step and was right in the Green Jacket's face. This odd boy she barely knew was risking everything for her, and she was just standing there like an idiot. Her hand stung where the squirrel had bitten her, sending twinges of pain up her wrist like it was being pricked with hot needles.

"Come on, then," Joey was shouting now, "what action are you going to take? You going to shoot me in front of a witness?"

"Yes," the Green Jacket replied, aiming his gun.

There was a blue flash, and Joey shot backwards, flattening the bracken and falling down the dip in the ground, out of sight. There was a rustle, a thud, then silence.

The Green Jacket turned his attention to Emma. "Now then, Miss Winrush. Are you going to come quietly or do I need restraints?"

"You shot him," was all Emma could say.

"He's just stunned. He'll wake up with the worst headache he's ever had. Maybe he'll think twice about interfering in the due process of the law in future. Now, come along. I've wasted enough time."

He holstered his gun, took Emma by the elbow and steered her along the forest path. She glanced back once, but she couldn't see Joey. As they walked, the Green Jacket spoke into his mobile.

"Operative Webb to Southport Control. Target Winrush secured and on my way in. ... No, no problem. She had a boyfriend with her but he is neutralised. ... What?" The Green Jacket, Webb, stopped dead, still keeping a firm grip on Emma's arm. "Seventeen, eighteen. White. Five ten, five eleven maybe… brown hair…" Webb listened intently into his phone, then let go of Emma's arm. "Stay here," he commanded. "Do *not* move, do you understand?"

Emma nodded and watched in confusion as Webb pulled his gun out again and hurried back over to the dip in the ground where Joey had fallen. He stopped at the top and looked around, then swore loudly and scrambled through the bracken and down. Emma wondered briefly if this might be a good opportunity for escape—even checked which of the paths might be the best one—but before she could decide, Webb appeared again, and he was furious.

"Where did he go?"

"Wh-who?" Emma stammered, genuinely bewildered.

"*Him*! Your boyfriend! Who the hell do you think? I saw you look back." Webb reached Emma and seized her by the arm, much more roughly this time. Pain shot through her as the squirrel bite made its presence felt again. "*Where did he go?*"

"He didn't go anywhere! My arm! You're hurting me!"

"Good," Webb snapped, leading her to the ridge where Joey had fallen. She stood, her whole arm throbbing now, and stared. She could see where she and Joey had hidden, but of Joey, there was no sign.

"If he didn't go anywhere..." Webb said through gritted teeth, but his voice sounded dull and distant. "Where the hell is he?"

Suddenly, Emma heard another voice speaking to her from somewhere close by.

"Go with him," it said.

She frowned, recognising the voice, but she couldn't quite place it. She looked around, but there was only Webb, raging not at her but into his phone now.

"Don't answer," the voice said, and Emma figured out the voice was speaking in her head. *"He can't hear. Just go with him, Emma. Everything will be fine. You will be looked after."*

As the voice spoke, Emma realised where she'd heard it before: on video clips taken on people's phones, back before she stopped mixing at school. She'd heard it on the answer-phone at home, when she'd called to leave messages her mum probably never listened to. It was the voice in her head—her own voice, but not the one she heard when she spoke. The one everyone else hears, and when you do actually hear it recorded somewhere, you think *do I really sound like that?*

Somehow, Emma was speaking to herself in her own head. That was when she began to wonder if maybe she was going insane.

Chapter Twelve

RAJ WOULD NEVER have imagined how pleased he was to see Radley and Hunt. He knew them both to be competent and committed, but while he liked Liza Hunt a great deal, he had his doubts about Billy Radley. He sometimes caught Radley looking at him with suspicion but didn't know whether it was because Raj was Asian, or because Raj was gay—or both—or merely because he'd stepped into the Catesby Foundation from pretty much nowhere and landed in a position of authority. Either way, there was a resentment at times. Radley never overstepped the mark, was never insubordinate, but it was there, whereas Liza was just pleasant to everyone and got on with the job in hand.

All the same, after spending rather too long crouched by the wheelie bin, Raj was delighted when he heard a car pull up nearby and heard Radley calling his name. He straightened up with some difficulty and jogged over to the car, an anonymous-looking Volvo. Radley already had the rear door open and helped him inside. Hunt waited until the door was closed, then took off, fast enough to get moving, but not so fast as to draw attention.

"You took your time," Raj said, once they were on their way.

"You're good at hiding," Liza Hunt replied, catching Raj's eye in the rear-view mirror. "I bet they used to hate you when you were a kid."

"They did." Raj laughed. "For lots of reasons."

"They got Geoff."

"I hoped he'd get away." Raj sighed. "I thought he might just do it."

"He's in the Royal, on a drip. They kicked seven shades of shite out of him. The doctors aren't sure if he'll make it. Still, you got away."

Raj looked at her through narrowed eyes. "Meaning?"

"Nothing. Just saying."

"So what else? Any news on Joey Cale?"

There was an uncomfortable pause. Neither Hunt nor Radley replied, like they were each waiting for the other to speak first.

"What's happened? Tell me."

"It could be nothing," Liza said. "Might be a tech issue. Probably is."

"Tell me," Raj repeated.

There was that pause again.

"He's gone off the grid," Radley said.

"What? He can't have. The tracker in his phone—"

"—is either not working, or we've lost the trace."

"This is great." Raj was furious. "I've waited six months for him to turn up and it's taken you lot six hours to lose him. What the hell happened?"

"It's not our fault," Hunt pointed out. "We had him pinned down in Freshfield woods. He was stationary, then the trace just...well, it just disappeared."

"Can't have done. It doesn't *just* do that. You could blow that phone up and the trace would still be there for a bit. So where's he gone? Has anyone been out there?"

"Yeah, oddly enough, Raj, we had that idea too," Radley said. "Field Unit called in. They found Joey's bag, but no Joey."

"His bag? That settles it. The Green Jackets must have got him."

"I don't think it's a simple as that. Witnesses saw a GJ at the scene, but he was taking a girl away. A girl, not Joey."

"A girl," Raj repeated. It wasn't a question. "A girl about Joey's age. Purple hair, maybe?"

"Sounds about right."

"A girl with purple hair who was supposed to be monitored at all times. For God's sake, the GJs have got Emma Winrush and you've lost Joey. This couldn't be a bigger cock-up if you'd planned it. What did they do with Joey's bag?"

"They brought it back. No mobile to be found."

"That's something." Raj thought for a moment. "As long as Joey's got his phone there's still a possibility of getting a trace at some point, so keep trying. For now, get me back to the Foundation as fast as you can. I need a shower and a change, and then I need to speak to Watson."

They drove on in silence for several miles, heading towards the city centre. The car bumped its way over potholes and disused tram tracks along a road which had once served the Liverpool docks and was now lined with scrap dealerships and recycling depots. A bit further on, a huge, empty warehouse reared up from the side of the road, a building which had once housed a large indoor market but was now largely derelict. Hunt drove the car through the entrance gateway and down a ramp into a parking area beneath the warehouse where several vehicles were already parked. She stopped the car, and the three of them got out.

Raj led the way to what must once have been an old fireplace of some kind, a hollow in the wall you probably would not even notice unless you were looking. Raj keyed a code into his phone; as soon as he pressed 'send', the wall slid away to reveal the brushed steel doors of a lift. They stepped inside, and Raj hit the button, sending the lift upwards.

At the top of the lift shaft, the doors opened, and the view changed considerably. Pristine white walls instead of dirty brick, and the rough floorboards of the warehouse were replaced with an immaculate laminate flooring. Waiting by the door were two men, both armed. They acknowledged Raj and his companions with a nod, then stepped aside to let them pass.

"I'll see you in fifteen at Watson's office," Raj said to Hunt and Radley. "I suggest you use the time to try again and find that trace. If we've lost both Joey and Emma, we're all going to be in a lot of trouble."

Raj didn't wait for an answer, just walked off leaving them there. He strode down several corridors, taking a left, then a right turn. He entered a code into a keypad next to a door on the left side of the corridor and went in.

It was hardly the room he'd been used to, back in the old world. His flat had been comfortably furnished; Raj had spent many hours going around markets and charity shops to find just the right sofa, the right chairs... Not the bed, though; that had to be new. Nowadays, he wondered if he would ever see the flat again. He'd been to the one belonging to the Raj of this world just once, to collect some clothes, but since he'd seen his double murdered, he stayed here, at the Merseyside Headquarters of the Catesby Foundation. The room was serviceable and as comfortable as it could be, but it wasn't home and never would be. Maybe one day...

Misha was waiting patiently inside Raj's quarters, and as soon as she saw him, the huge dog bundled into him, nearly knocking him off his feet. He sat with her for a few minutes, enjoying the feel of her fur under his hands, then grabbed a tin of dog food and tipped the contents into her bowl. Misha looked at the bowl, then looked at Raj and wagged her tail.

"Sorry, girl. Can't stay. I'll give you a walk later. Promise."

Reluctantly, he left her, stripped off his grimy clothes and ran the shower as hot as he could. He stayed under it long enough to clean himself thoroughly, although the stench of the wheelie bin still clung to the inside of his nostrils.

He dressed quickly in clean clothes and headed back along the corridor, past the lift in which he had arrived, to a door at the end, this one again flanked by two guards. Hunt was waiting outside the room already, and Radley was hurrying towards them from the other direction. Raj nodded to Hunt and pushed the door open.

Sitting behind a desk, talking on the phone, was a striking woman in her fifties. Her platinum-grey hair was tied back in a tight plait, and even her military-style fatigues looked brand-new. Whomever she was speaking to on the phone was clearly getting a hard time of it.

"I don't care! I want him looked after. If he dies, you'd better start running." Davina Watson hung up the phone and sat back in her chair. "The hospital," she explained to those in the room. "They don't think Geoff is going to pull through. I shouldn't have been so hard. I'm sure they're doing all they can."

"I'm sorry," Raj said. "Geoff's a good man."

"We all take our chances."

"I should have stayed. I shouldn't have left him there."

"And we'd have been burying both of you. You didn't have a choice, Raj." Watson sounded exhausted but tried, briefly, to smile. She gave up, and the smile dropped from her face. "This is all going wrong. First Geoff, then they took Emma Winrush and now Joey Cale has gone missing. I hope this Joey is worth it, Raj, because all this has started since he turned up."

"He is," Raj assured her. "You *know* why he's important. If it's the same Joey Cale I knew, and it certainly looks like it, then he was the answer before. He might well be the answer again."

"Then you'd better find him, hadn't you? We've worked too long and too hard for it all to come crashing down around our ears now."

"I'll do what I can."

"Do better than that," Watson said. "Find Joey Cale and find him fast."

Chapter Thirteen

JOEY HAD NO idea where he was. It was dark, that was certain. It was also cold and damp. One minute, he'd been standing in the woods with the Green Jacket pointing a gun at him, the next, there had been a bright blue flash, Joey's heart jumped, and suddenly he was here—wherever 'here' was—feeling like he'd been kicked in the sternum by a horse. And he was on his own. There was no sign of Emma or the Green Jacket, so Joey had clearly gone somewhere they hadn't.

It appeared to be a tunnel of some kind; the floor felt and sounded like stone under his feet. When he reached out a hand, he could feel a rough stone wall, with water—at least, he hoped it was water—dripping down it. He could also hear a dripping somewhere nearby. He felt around for the rucksack, remembering it had a torch in it, but wherever he was, the bag hadn't arrived with him.

Although is was dark, it wasn't pitch-black; there was a dim source of light coming from somewhere. It had a strange reddish tinge to it, but, Joey reasoned, if there was light, it might mean the tunnel wasn't completely enclosed, in which case there was really only one thing to do: follow the light source and see where it was coming from.

There was a strange smell in the tunnel, too. It was an acrid smell, as if something had been burning, and it seemed familiar in some way, though Joey couldn't quite figure out why. It wasn't quite like burning wood or paper—more like the bottom of a saucepan that had boiled dry. Whatever it was, Joey was in no particular hurry to find out where it was coming from.

Slowly, with one hand on the tunnel wall, he moved through the gloom, testing one foot in front of the other in case there were any unseen obstacles for him to trip over. He was unable to see his feet or the tunnel floor and just had to go carefully, trusting there were no holes or loose rocks in his way. The light was still there, but no brighter as yet.

As Joey cautiously felt his way along, his foot suddenly touched something soft, which moved, breaking the silence of the tunnel with the skittering of claws on stone. *Oh, great. There are rats in here.* He shuddered and sped up as much as he dared.

Luckily, no further wildlife made its presence felt, and gradually the light grew a little brighter. It still wasn't enough to help his vision greatly, but instead painted the tunnel walls in an unearthly shade of crimson. The smell was getting stronger too, and it stung the back of his nose and throat. He pulled the collar of his coat up and raised the zip to the top in an attempt to block out the smell, which helped to an extent. He tried holding his breath, but that didn't help much either; when he had to breathe, he caught a lungful of the foul air and coughed so violently he had to stop walking for a minute to catch his breath. As the coughing subsided, he heard something, a noise from up ahead. He hoped it was merely his echo. If it wasn't, somebody up ahead had just spoken.

Joey stayed still and listened. Then, just as he'd convinced himself the tunnel was playing tricks with his hearing, he heard it again.

"*Who's there*?"

Joey didn't dare to move. The voice, if that was indeed what he had heard, was hardly audible and barely human. It was cracked and guttural, more of a croak. Joey waited, just in case he was hearing things, and then it came again.

"*Who's there*?"

Joey was torn between concern that someone might be in trouble and need help, and a desire to run as fast as he could in the opposite direction. There was a part of him that was curious to know who had spoken, but a bigger part of him really, really didn't want to know. Then the voice said something that settled it.

"*I know you.*"

Joey should have run. He should have put as much distance as he could between himself and that hideous voice. But curiosity got the better of him, and instead, he walked towards it. As he did so, the tunnel wall fell away under his hand, and he was suddenly in a large cavern—a cavern which proved to contain the sources of the light, the stench and the voice. In the middle of the cavern was a pile of rocks, on top of which something smouldered like a fire that had been left to go out on its own. Joey crept towards it.

"*Closer,*" the voice said. "*Let me see you.*"

It seemed to be coming from somewhere right next to the fire. Joey moved closer and then stopped, his brain unable to process what his eyes were seeing. The fire was not a fire. It was a mound of burning coals in the rough shape of a man and looked for all the world like the remains of someone who had burnt to death. Then it moved, and Joey jumped back so quickly he stumbled. What had been the head of the person turned with a noise like two stones scraping together and looked at him. Joey could make out the blackened shape of the skull, cinders still burning in the eye sockets.

"*Joey Cale,*" it said. "*I knew.*"

That was when, once again, Joey felt his heart stop.

Chapter Fourteen

AROUND THE TIME Emma Winrush was getting to school and Joey Cale was staring out across the Mersey, Richard Wells flashed his pass at the security personnel and entered Ground Zero.

Ground Zero.

You had no idea of the scale of it unless you actually saw it, and very few people saw it. High fences had rapidly been erected after the disaster, and a rigidly enforced air exclusion zone ensured that few bird's eye images had been seen. Some grainy footage from drones had appeared briefly on the internet before the ban, but they had quickly been removed and any further drones were shot out of the sky as soon as they were sighted. All the general public could see of Trafalgar Square now was the fences and armed police everywhere. Once the grief and outcry had subsided, the fences and police were accepted as part of life, and people stopped noticing.

That, Richard Wells thought, was probably for the best. He had never got used to the sights he had seen inside the fences and probably never would. And yet it was his job to oversee the activity within the cordon. At first, he'd been honoured when he was asked to head up the Government Select Committee overseeing the investigation and ultimately the rebuilding programme. Now he knew what had really gone on behind the fences, and that he wasn't actually in charge of anything at all, he wished he had never agreed. But still, he had to put on his hard hat and hi-vis and come here most days. If the public knew what was going on behind the fence, they would be every bit as concerned as he was.

The disaster had completely removed Trafalgar Square from the map. There was nothing left. The iconic images everyone had seen over and over again of Nelson's Column descending like a demolished factory chimney was only part of it. The explosion had obliterated the Square, ripped up the ground and crippled the Tube lines underneath, and while many people had died above ground, hundreds had perished below. Nine months later and bodies were still being recovered, many more still unaccounted for.

This was Richard Wells' workplace. This was what he had to see most days, and it haunted his dreams. It wasn't so much the absence of the Square and its iconic Column that bothered him; it was the excavation under the ground and the fact it wasn't just corpses they were looking for. Somewhere down there was the cause of all this, and Wells wasn't sure he wanted to be around when they found it.

This morning, a light rain was falling, adding an air of gloom to the already grim scene as Wells was greeted by Martin Buxton, once Deputy Commissioner of the Met and now leading the investigation. The two men shook hands; Buxton's was icy cold.

"Any news?" Wells asked. "Good or bad?"

"Not today. Not so far. God knows what they're doing down there."

"I don't think God has much to do with this." Wells surveyed the scene.

"That's not what they say."

"I'm not interested in what the cranks say." Wells' voice was firm and official—the one he used to cover his doubts. "People did this, Martin. People I'd love to see caught and executed at the Tower, like they always used to do to traitors."

"I agree," Buxton said. "But probably best not make that the official line."

"Brought to justice is the official line. The public want to see someone, anyone brought to justice. But seriously, can you see it happening? Whichever bastards did this blew themselves to bits along with everyone else. They're not going to find anything down there apart from pieces of innocent people."

"Yes, well, that's not what *they* say." Buxton dropped his voice to little more than a whisper and looked around to make sure he wasn't overheard. "Speaking of which, apparently *she* is going to be on site today, looking over our shoulders."

"That's all we need."

"What is all you need, Mr. Wells?" a voice enquired. Wells jumped like he had been caught smoking at school.

Standing behind him, flanked by two enormous armed officers with Kevlar vests under their green coats, was the subject of the conversation. Standing a good foot shorter than the men either side of her, she was dressed in a long, black leather coat, her dark hair scraped back into a severe ponytail, a pair of sunglasses perched on top of her head, completely unnecessary in this rain.

"Ms. Mallory," Wells said. "I was just-ah-remarking that this weather is all we need."

"The weather," the woman replied, her voice betraying no emotion. "A conversation about the weather. Are there not more important things to discuss? Like, for example, whether this vital and very expensive investigation is actually getting anywhere?"

"I was just bringing Mr. Wells up to speed," Buxton interjected. "As I understand it, there has been little progress in the past day or so."

"That is what you told me last week and the week before. I'm starting to wonder, Mr. Buxton, if we have the right people in charge of this job. And higher individuals than me are wondering the same."

"With respect," Buxton argued, "we cannot find something that isn't there, no matter how deep we dig. The initial reports suggested nothing survived the explosion and that has, in my opinion, not changed."

"*With respect*," Mallory said, "you know as well as I do, we have information to suggest otherwise. Now, I have been tasked with informing you gentlemen that you need to get results and get them fast, or, as I understand it, your careers will be among the things this disaster has buried."

Without another word, Anna Mallory and her two silent minders stalked away.

Buxton and Wells exchanged a look of resignation, and not for the first time. Before either could speak, Buxton's mobile rang.

"Yes?" he snapped. "Yes it is. … You've… Right. Don't touch anything. We'll be right there."

He hung up and looked at Wells, who saw a mixture of excitement and fear in his associate's eyes.

"We need to get down there," Buxton said. "There's something you have to see."

Chapter Fifteen

Emma had lost track of how long they had been travelling and had no idea where she was.

After Joey had been shot, the Green Jacket, Webb or whatever his name was, had led her at gunpoint through the woods and to a black van, with blacked-out windows, parked awkwardly near the snack stand. Or not so much parked as abandoned, but as the van belonged to the Green Jackets and one of Webb's colleagues was in the driver's seat, nobody was arguing.

Emma had a headache, but she hadn't heard any more voices in her head since Joey got shot and was now starting to wonder if she had heard any at all. The whole thing had left her feeling so shaken that, when Webb opened the back of the van and told her to get in, she did so without question.

Inside, there was a bench on either side, with a rail attached to the wall above each bench. The van was clearly intended to convey prisoners who would be cuffed to the rails. Luckily, Emma didn't seem worthy of cuffs so just sat on one of the benches, which was uncomfortable enough without cuffs; the rail dug into her back just above her shoulder blades. It was also dark, once Webb slammed the door shut, with only minimal light coming through the blanked-out windows in the back door. All Emma could do was sit and wait as the van drove off to God only knew where.

Her hand hurt. The site of the squirrel bite was hot and throbbed painfully, shooting shards of pain up her arm. She thought it was probably infected, but she couldn't see well enough to check, so she kept the improvised dressing where it was and hoped that wherever they were going, there'd be someone who could look at it before the infection made its way any further into her bloodstream.

On they drove. There was no communication from the two Green Jackets in the front, so Emma just sat there, bored, scared and in pain, wondering what she had ever done to deserve this. She had always tried to be good. Her parents had always said she never caused them any trouble when she was young. Even after her dad went off with his new woman, leaving his daughter with a mum hell-bent on slowly drinking herself to death, Emma tried not to be any bother. She didn't want to be the cause of any more stress, so she got on with what she had to do without complaining.

There was nothing she had ever done, or would ever consider doing, that would bring her to the attention of the Green Jackets. She had never so much as shoplifted a chocolate bar, let alone become involved in anything to make the Government's guard dogs take notice of her. That was what scared her the most: how could she defend herself when she had no idea what she was supposed to have done?

By Emma's reckoning, they had been driving for maybe a couple of hours before the van finally stopped, which meant they could be just about anywhere—Birmingham maybe? She really had no clue. Even when the back door opened and Webb and his colleague told her to get out, she was still none the wiser. The van had pulled up in what looked like an underground car park, and the only vehicles in it were anonymous four-by-fours and vans, all black or white and with tinted windows.

"Where are we?" she asked, moving her legs and shoulders, which had stiffened up during the journey. She didn't really expect an answer and wasn't altogether surprised when Webb took her by the arm and led her to a lift door. He pressed the button and, when the door slid open, pushed her inside. His colleague, for some reason, didn't follow.

The lift went up three floors. When the door opened again, Webb led her down a dismal, grey-painted corridor. They stopped outside a blank door with no handle or lock. Webb placed his hand on a panel at the side of it; there was a *clunk* from the door, and Webb pushed it open.

"Get in there and wait," he said.

Emma mutely did as she was told, and the door closed with Webb on the other side of it. Once again, Emma was on her own in what was obviously a cell. There was a rough padded seat bolted to the wall opposite the door and a covered bucket in one corner which she didn't dare investigate further. Other than that, the room was empty. The only improvement on the van was a dim light in the ceiling.

Emma sat on the uncomfortable seat. She wanted to cry and may well have done so had she not heard a voice again.

"*Emma Winrush.*"

It seemed to come from everywhere and nowhere. It was vaguely male, but scarcely human and nothing like her own. It sounded like the voice of an alien in a bad film.

"*Emma Winrush,*" it said again. The bite on Emma's hand pulsed in time with the words.

"*You're not the right Emma Winrush, of course—*" Emma heard the echo of a laugh in her head "*—but you may have to do.*"

"Who are you?" Emma tried to ask out loud, but her voice came out as little more than a squeak. She sounded pathetic and knew it.

"*You will know me soon enough. I am keen to see you again.*"

"What do you mean? Who—"

"*I killed you last time,*" hissed the voice with barely concealed, obscene glee. "*But this time, I will claim you. It has already begun.*"

Then it was gone, leaving Emma shaken and terrified, on her own in the cell. Now she couldn't stop herself. She curled up on the seat and wept.

Chapter Sixteen

RAJ WAS MOBILE again, driving as fast as the traffic would allow. It was late afternoon, and everyone seemed to be leaving the city centre at once, so there was no chance of him breaking the speed limit even if he'd wanted to. In any case, the last thing he wanted was to draw attention to himself. So he let the car stop and start, speed up and slow down, just like everyone else.

Beside him in the passenger seat, Liza Hunt stared at the tablet in her hand. The screen showed a map of Merseyside, and there was a pinprick of light flashing at a location just up the coast.

"Any movement?" Raj asked.

"Static at the moment," Hunt replied.

"And you're sure it's him?"

"That's eight."

"Eight what?"

"Eight times you've asked me. Yes, it is definitely Joey Cale's phone. If it's Joey Cale holding it, I don't know."

"Someone could have found it," Raj suggested. "And yes, I know we've had this conversation before. But they could have."

"All I know is the trace disappeared and now it's back. We'll know when we get there."

"Formby?"

"Formby. It hasn't moved far, if at all."

Raj muttered under his breath as another car pulled into his lane in front of him without indicating. In his inside jacket pocket, his mobile started ringing. Keeping one hand on the steering wheel and his eyes out front, he fished his phone out and tossed it to Hunt.

"Answer that for us, Liza. If it's the wife, tell her I won't be home for my tea."

Hunt flashed him a smile, said, "That'll be the day," and hit the answer icon.

"Raj's phone," she said, but then all humour left her voice and she mouthed *Davina* at Raj. "No, he's driving. ... No, we're, what, half an hour away. Maybe more in this traffic. ...What? ... When? ...Okay, I'll tell him." Hunt hung up and passed the phone back to Raj.

"Problem?" he asked.

"Maybe. Davina says get Joey—"

"If it's him."

"—*if* it's him, and get back ASAP. Word from London is it's all kicking off down there. Sounds like earlier today they found something."

"Shit," Raj muttered. "Of all the times... Did she say what?"

"No, just that."

"Okay. Try ringing Joey's phone again."

"He didn't answer last time. Or the time before."

"One more try."

Hunt shrugged and took Raj's phone back off him. She thumbed the screen and made the call. Raj, still concentrating on the road, saw out of the corner of his eye that she was shaking her head.

"He's not answering."

"Keep trying," Raj said, as the traffic began to flow again. "Hopefully we'll be there before his battery runs out."

Even if they weren't moving quickly, they were at least moving. Hunt kept trying Joey's mobile, without success. Raj kept driving, his attention on the other cars, constantly looking out for plain black or white vans with tinted windows, but he saw nothing suspicious, not until they were nearly there.

The dual carriageway which bypassed Formby village was busy as ever, and if the traffic had been moving any faster, Raj might not have noticed the unmarked white van some yards ahead, half concealed in an overgrown turn-off, but at the speed they were going, he saw it well in time. He swore, indicated and pulled into the outside lane, keeping pace with a tatty maroon people carrier ferrying a party of kids and concealing Raj from shades-wearing eyes until he had safely passed. He eased back into the inside lane and turned off at the next roundabout, heading for the pine woods and, hopefully, Joey Cale.

Raj parked up and, while Hunt tried Joey's phone yet again, went over to the snack stand.

"Hi. Black coffee, please," he said, then, "Been busy today?"

"Steady," the man on the stand replied, pouring Raj's drink.

"Someone said the Jackets were here earlier." Raj made it sound casual, like it was just something he'd heard somewhere.

"Yeah. Took some girl away."

"Just a girl?"

"That's all I saw." The man was cautious now.

"Bloody anarchists." Raj took his coffee. "Starting them younger all the time."

It was clear the coffee-seller was going to say no more, so Raj went back to Hunt. He sipped the coffee, grimaced and threw the cup and the rest in the bin.

"The Jackets have got Emma. So that's her accounted for. The guy said they just took a girl—Joey must be here somewhere."

"Best go and find him then," Hunt said and headed off towards the woods. Raj smiled despite himself and followed.

Once under the canopy of trees, Raj called Joey's name, paused for a response, but when he received no reply called again.

"Hang on. Let's give this a try." Hunt took out Raj's mobile and dialled Joey's number.

"Seriously? You think he's going to answer now?"

"*Listen*," Hunt insisted. Somewhere, not far away, the Amstrad mobile ringtone was chiming.

"Got him!" Raj said triumphantly.

"Hey! It was my..." Hunt began, but Raj had already taken off through the trees in the direction of the ringing phone. By the time she caught up with him, he was standing at the foot of one of the bigger pine trees. "Is that him?" she asked.

Raj stared down at the body lying on the pine needles, the ringing mobile phone at its side. Joey's eyes were closed, his face deathly pale, and a trickle of blood ran from his left nostril.

"I think we're too late."

Chapter Seventeen

RICHARD WELLS FLIPPED the switch to turn on the light on his hard hat and followed Buxton down the steps leading below Ground Zero. The steps had been constructed specifically to take service personnel down below the ground and had presumably passed all kinds of safety tests, but Wells, who was mildly claustrophobic at the best of times, felt them wobble beneath his feet and didn't feel safe at all.

Behind him, light leaked in from the hole in the ground, and he could see the glare of the halogen lamps set up to illuminate the excavation site, but the steps themselves were lit only by his head torch, and he held tightly onto the handrail as he carefully took one step at a time. Ahead of him, Buxton's hi-vis receded into the distance; Buxton was usually a man in a hurry, but the prospect of a discovery was practically making him skip down the steps like a mountain goat.

When Wells finally caught up, Buxton was already deep in conversation with two other people. Wells recognised one straight away: Les Cox, foreman of the excavation crew. His sheer size made him unmistakable. He was tall and broad, and not for the first time, Wells wondered how the makeshift staircase held his weight at all. The other person was a slim woman who was younger than Cox—mid-to-late thirties was Wells' guess. Her short, red hair was tucked up under her hard hat, and she looked entirely unused to wearing one. Wells thought she seemed familiar, and he had a vague idea he might have seen her being interviewed on TV.

Buxton made the introductions. "This is Richard Wells, Head of the Select Committee overseeing this project. Richard, I'm sure you don't need me to introduce Carla Lockhart."

Of course, Wells thought, smiling as if there had never been any doubt. She was the go-to archaeologist whenever the BBC News needed someone rather more glamorous and American than the usual grey academics.

"Carla, good to see you," he said, using his politician's handshake. "What have we got?"

"I haven't confirmed it as yet," Lockhart consulted the notes she was carrying on a clipboard, "but it appears to be the remains of a body."

"A body? Surely that's more Martin's domain than yours."

"Not this one," Buxton answered. "This isn't one of the casualties. It appears to have been unearthed by the blast. They actually found it yesterday, but I've been waiting for Carla to get here and authenticate it before bringing you in."

"Why? What is it?" Wells was impatient and irritated he hadn't been advised about the find sooner. "Why wait? I should have been told about this straight away."

"Easier to show you than explain," Buxton said. "When you see it, I think you'll understand why a phone call wouldn't do, and why I needed an expert to have look at it first. It's this way."

Buxton let Les Cox lead, Carla Lockhart following in his wake. As they walked, Wells realised they were going down a tunnel, and there were rail tracks beneath his feet.

"What is this? An old Tube line?"

"There are lots of them." Cox spoke for the first time. "Some not used anymore, some, like this one, never completed and abandoned."

"Abandoned? Why?"

"Lots of reasons. If it hadn't been for the explosion making a wall collapse, no-one would have remembered it was here at all. And if the wall hadn't collapsed, we'd never have found…well… what we found."

It dawned on Wells why this area of the excavation was different to others he had seen. Normally, the place was buzzing with members of the emergency services and the rescue crews, but in this section, although it was clear work had been going on, there was no sign of activity at all.

"Where is everyone?" he asked.

"Soon as we found it, we evacuated the area," Buxton told him. "Only essential personnel have seen this, and we need to keep it that way. The last thing we need is some camera-happy fireman putting it all over social media. This is potentially way too big for that."

Cox and Lockhart had stopped and were looking at a section of wall.

"Here it is," Buxton said. "The blast brought the tiles and half the brickwork down. It appears to have been buried in the earth behind the bricks."

Wells directed his helmet light to the wall. At first, he couldn't quite comprehend what he was looking at. It appeared as if the figure of a person was imprinted into the wall, but as he looked closer, he saw within the imprint were the remains of bones, and a partial skull. But that wasn't all…

"Is that…" he began but found he couldn't finish the sentence. The words just would not come.

"It certainly appears that way," Lockhart responded. "I need to get the bone fragments carbon-dated, but it's old. Very old. It's virtually fossilised, but the clay in the soil has preserved it. It looks to me like it might have been buried in the ground for thousands of years. If they had dug just a little further when the tunnel was built, they would have found it then and someone else would have been having this conversation."

"But how is that even possible?" Wells asked, and then, when he could no longer avoid the obvious question, added, "And are those…?"

"Well, I thought, at first—we all did—that other things had been buried here with it, but no. They certainly seem to be attached."

"But…but…those are *wings*!"

Lockhart took a step closer to the figure embedded in the wall and let her torch play across the ancient, soil-encrusted feathers.

"Yes," she replied. "Yes, they are. So either we're looking at some strange humanoid bird we've never come across before, or…"

"Or?"

"Or we've just stumbled across the corpse of an angel."

Chapter Eighteen

When Joey opened his eyes, his immediate feeling was one of complete disorientation. He'd expected to find the stone floor of the tunnel under his back or—if what he'd just experienced had been some kind of bad dream—to be back in the woods, lying on twigs and pine needles. The last thing he expected was that he would be lying in rather more comfort than that, on the back seat of a moving car. Head spinning, he tried to sit up, but dizziness overtook him and he slumped back down again.

"Whoa, take it easy," a voice said, and Joey recognised it straight away.

"Raj," he croaked, his throat so dry he could hardly speak.

"Welcome back. I can't wait to hear where you've been. Liza Hunt—" he addressed someone Joey couldn't see "—meet the famous Joey Cale."

"Hi," said a female voice from the driver's seat. "We'll meet properly in a minute. Nearly there."

"Emma," Joey said. "What happened to Emma? Is she okay?"

"Just try and get some rest," Raj replied. "We'll fill you in when we get there."

Joey lay back and closed his eyes. He was still feeling woozy, like he had just woken from a very deep sleep, and his heart was beating a syncopated rhythm. He tried to concentrate on breathing steadily, and gradually his heart settled down. By the time the car stopped, it felt almost normal again.

Once the engine had been switched off, the door next to Joey's head opened, and Raj's hands slid under his shoulders. "Come on, sit up."

Joey rested his head on his friend's shoulder for a moment, then managed to get up into a sitting position. The effort made him light-headed, and he was greatly relieved when Raj handed him a bottle of water. Joey gulped it greedily and nearly choked.

"*Sip it,* Joey," Raj instructed.

"Thanks," said Joey, his voice sounding more like his own. "I needed that."

"Think you can walk? It's not far."

"Should be okay. Just need to find my legs."

He carefully swung his feet out of the car. Using the doorframe for support, he pulled himself up until he was more or less upright. He waited until he was sure his legs were not going to give way, then let go of the doorframe and stood unaided. Raj hovered next to him ready to offer help, but it wasn't needed.

Joey took in his surroundings. They'd stopped in some kind of underground car park—the kind of place where, in bad thriller movies, the villains took people to shoot them. A tall, attractive woman who looked to be in her late twenties or early thirties climbed out of the driver's seat and came over, a smile on her face and her hand extended.

"Liza," she said.

"Joey," he replied and shook her hand.

"Well, this is nice," Raj said, "but we'd better get you inside. Liza, could you get rid of the car please?"

"No problem." She smiled at Joey again. "See you in a bit."

"This way." Raj led Joey to a lift and once they were inside and ascending, turned to him with a grin. "Good to have you back. But where the hell did you go?"

"I don't know. I got shot and went—*somewhere*—but I don't know where. It was like a tunnel, and there was a body burning on a pile of rocks."

"A body?" Raj was visibly shocked. "You mean a corpse?"

"I thought so. But then it spoke. It knew me, Raj. It knew who I was. Then I woke up in your car."

Raj must've caught the look of consternation on Joey's face as he stepped out of the lift. "Yes, I know. Bit different once you get inside. As far as anyone's concerned, this is a telemarketing company. Kind of makes us invisible. So, let's get this straight. A burning corpse spoke to you. Did it address you by name?"

"Yes. It said…let me think… 'Joey Cale. I knew.' Like that. Like it had been expecting me."

Raj frowned. "I don't like the sound of a burning man. Makes me think of that thing your mate Saunders turned into."

"Not my mate," Joey muttered. Then he paused. "That's it," he said. "I think it *was* Saunders."

"*What?* No. It can't be. Saunders is dead. Emma got him. Crowbar in the chest. We saw it."

"We saw him go through the portal, Raj. We never saw him die. Saunders is a demon or whatever. Who knows what it takes to kill him?"

"Point," Raj said as they stopped outside a door. Joey was a little disturbed to see it was being guarded by two armed men. "Anyway, here we are. Welcome to the Catesby Foundation. You're about to meet Davina Watson, head of the Foundation, well, this branch anyway. Don't worry. She only *looks* like she'd eat you alive."

"What's the Catesby—"

"All will become clear. I'll let Davina explain."

Raj knocked on the door, and when a voice called, "Come," he opened the door and ushered Joey inside.

Davina Watson, Joey assumed, sat behind her desk, working on something on her computer, and raised a hand to ask them to wait. She finished what she was doing, then pushed the monitor to one side.

"Raj," she acknowledged. "And you must be Joey. Welcome. Forgive me for not getting up."

As she said that, Joey noticed the seat she was sitting in was in fact a wheelchair.

"Raj, can you organise some drinks? I could do with a coffee and I'm sure Joey could too. Maybe a sandwich as well?"

Raj nodded and left the room. Watson gestured to a comfortable-looking padded chair on the other side of the desk, and Joey sat.

"I must apologise in advance," she said. "You're going to have to take a lot of information on board in a short space of time. Has Raj told you anything about us?"

"No. We haven't really had a chance."

"Okay. The quick version. The Catesby Foundation has existed in one form or another since the time of the Gunpowder Plot, hence the name. Robert Catesby was the real brains behind the plot. Guy Fawkes just gets the parties in his honour. The Foundation has sometimes just been a couple of people, sometimes more, depending on the need. Over the past decade or so, it has grown considerably, because we believe the need is probably greater than it has ever been."

"I'm sorry," Joey interrupted. "The need for what?"

"The Foundation monitors the government of the day. Doesn't matter which party is in power. We keep an eye on it on behalf of the people. Governments can get above themselves, and it's up to us to see that doesn't happen. There are branches in most areas of the country. For my sins, I head up this one. I understand you're not from this world, though. There may be a Catesby Foundation where you're from, who knows? Tell me, did Trafalgar Square happen in your world?"

Joey was a bit thrown by the casual way in which Watson referred to him being from another world. It was still something he was getting used to, but she seemed to be way ahead of him.

"No," he said.

"I bet you don't have the Green Jackets either."

"Only in the army, I think, but that's something different."

"I thought not. The Green Jackets were set up in direct response to Trafalgar Square. And that's really the point. We don't believe that the destruction of Nelson's Column had anything at all to do with anarchists or terrorists, as the Government claim. The internet is full of theories, but the most popular one is that the Government has simply used it to establish an authoritarian hold on the country, with the Green Jackets as their guard dogs. It's a very dangerous situation because it paints us as precisely the sort of anarchists they claim to be hunting. In the meantime, we know the Government is trying to find out exactly what did happen in Trafalgar Square, and so are we."

"What do you think happened?"

"The public has seen plenty of videos played time and time again which claim to show that a bomb detonated at the base of the Column. They have been shown photographs in the newspapers. Everyone watched the footage, and it has become engrained in the public consciousness."

Joey understood this. He was only young when the Twin Towers came down in his world, but his dad had told him how everyone had been glued to their televisions that day, watching the plane hit the tower over and over again, like if they watched it often enough, one time the planes would miss and it would not have happened.

"The footage was faked," Watson said. "That's what we believe. We have seen real pictures before they were all suppressed. It's pretty clear that whatever hit Trafalgar Square came from above. Something crashed there. Something came from somewhere else and crashed onto Trafalgar Square."

Chapter Nineteen

FOUR P.M. WAS changeover time for the guards of Cell 14. Fox had been on since eight a.m., and apart from an entertaining half hour when the prisoner had put up a fight as he took her lunch in, it had been an uneventful day. He was relieved then, when Buckler came strolling down the corridor to take over. Buckler never seemed to hurry anywhere. Even on the rare occasions when there was an emergency, he ambled along, his long legs getting him there just as quickly as any of his running colleagues.

"Any trouble?" he asked as he approached.

"Nah," Fox reported. "She didn't like the look of her lunch so I had to calm her down a bit, but nothing since."

"Not surprised with the food here," Buckler said. "Wouldn't give it to the dog. Go on then, mate, do one."

Fox grinned and headed down the corridor, leaving Buckler outside the cell. Buckler flipped down the viewing hatch in the door. The prisoner sat huddled up on the bench holding her right arm. *That must have been what Fox meant by calming her down*, Buckler thought. *Vicious bastard.*

***

Inside the cell, the prisoner massaged her arm. When she had made a casual remark about not liking the look of the food, the guard had dropped the tray on the floor and told her to clear it up. She hadn't done it quickly enough, so he'd twisted her arm behind her back and pushed her hard into the wall. The arm was bruised at best, possibly sprained. She continued to massage, feeling heat seep into the ache.

She had no idea how long it was since she'd been taken. She had worked out early on that the lights were operated in an irregular way; the inconsistency of the length of days that created was obviously intended to keep her disorientated. It worked. She slept badly and had lost all concept of time, so she could have been in this cell for a couple of months, or it might only have been weeks. She hadn't been charged with anything, nor seen a solicitor, barely even been questioned. She had just been left in this cell to rot and fed on crap several times a day.

Every now and then, she was allowed to shower—only when a female guard was on duty—and walk up and down the corridor by way of exercise, but there was never any conversation from the guards who walked her or washed her. She had no clue as to why she was being held or what was going to happen to her or when.

In the end, she had been taken far too easily. In spite of all the warnings and the training, she hadn't spotted she was being tailed until it was too late. It wasn't even the Green Jackets who had taken her, but a couple who looked for all the world like they were out on a date. They had passed her on the street, then stopped in front of her and that was that. The cuffs were on, and she was bundled into the back of a car parked around the corner. It was a fast, clinical, but above all targeted take-down. They knew exactly who she was.

Now, she was stuck here, in this cell, and could only hope someone knew where she was and was doing something about it. She just wished they'd bloody well hurry up.

The heat from her hand had sorted the pain out, and sprained or not, her arm was now fine. She carried on holding it, though. She didn't know whether her captors knew what she could do, so she kept up the pretence a while longer in case prying eyes were watching. She had long suspected there was a camera somewhere in the cell, and who knew what might happen if it became apparent she could heal with a touch? Or maybe they already knew. Maybe that was why the guards were allowed to treat her as brutally as they sometimes did without anyone being in the least bit concerned about any injuries she might have incurred.

Maybe this was what she deserved for the mistakes she had made. For too long, she had spent her off-shift hours drinking and partying with anyone who would join her. But the hours she spent tending to patients in the hospital were sometimes so grim she had to let off steam somehow. Only when she'd become lost in a version of her own world that was mostly empty of people was she able to break free of the routine killing her soul.

At first, the temptation of too much booze lying around with no-one to claim it had been too much to resist. The fact that the first person she met was a loser didn't help much. There was nothing else to do but drink—and the other stuff she really didn't want to think about now—but all that had changed when she met Joey Cale, Emma Winrush and the two kids they were looking after. *Then* she knew she wanted to change, and somehow she had the power to do so. She'd saved Joey, but she couldn't save Emma; she couldn't heal the dead.

Passing through the portal Joey had somehow created was like having her guts ripped out and put back in the wrong order. That and the fact she was apparently back where she'd come from had disorientated her. Finding out it wasn't the world she thought it was but one very like it confused her even more, but the last straw was learning Raj was already here, and had been for a couple of months, somehow. He worked with some underground organisation.

She'd wanted to run, and keep running, especially when she started seeing news reports that featured prominently another woman with her face and her name. Maybe if she had followed her instincts and made a run for it, disappeared somewhere, she wouldn't be stuck in this cell with an endless routine of nothing.

It came as a shock, then, when she heard the key turn in the lock. The guards had only just changed, and that usually meant a good few hours—as far as she could estimate—before the next crap meal was due. But the door was being opened, and her stomach was churning. Either she was being freed or things were about to get worse. When she saw who was on the other side of the door, she knew immediately it was the latter.

Standing in the corridor, with an armed and helmeted guard at either shoulder, was the woman who wore her face—the one in charge of the green-coated thugs who now seemed to run the country.

"On your feet," the other Anna Mallory snapped. "And don't think about trying to run or we'll see how fast you can heal yourself if your kneecaps are shot out."

"What do you want with me?" She tried to sound defiant and was ashamed by the pitiful way her voice came out.

"You're coming with me," came the reply. "And then you're going on a little road trip. We've got a job for you. It's probably—no, *definitely*—the most important job you'll ever do."

Chapter Twenty

From her own cell, a little further down the corridor, Emma heard there was something going on. She could hear voices but couldn't make out what they were saying. It was hard to concentrate through the haze of pain, and the voices floating in an out of her head made it impossible to tell what was real and what was not.

Her bitten hand—in fact her whole arm—felt like it was on fire. She could almost feel the infection pulsing through her veins like hot oil and knew if she didn't get antibiotics or something soon, she'd be in real trouble. But even though she had asked the guard, when he had brought the food that sat untouched on the bench beside her, nobody had come to look at her hand, and now she feared nobody would. She could picture the infection creeping insidiously through her body, turning her blood to pus, and wondered if she would be left to die here.

It was obviously making her hallucinate, or whatever the word was for things you could hear but not see. That was the only logical explanation for the voices she kept hearing, two of them: the rustling, rasping, horrible one that kept saying it was her master, and the other one, quieter but insistent, that sounded a bit like her. She hated the first one, while the second one just got on her nerves; she wished they'd both shut up and let her think.

She still didn't have a clue why the Green Jackets had been looking for her in the first place. She'd never done anything wrong, never attended any of the anti-Government marches, never posted any political opinions online. There was nothing in her past that would make the Green Jackets even remotely interested in her. Yet they had come to the school and then tracked her to the woods. Now, they had her, locked up tight in a cell, and no-one was coming anywhere near her to accuse her of whatever and let her fight her corner. She wished they'd get on with it so she could deny it—because that was the truth—and then maybe let her go.

You will be looked after, the voice that sounded like her had said. That was a laugh. Nobody was looking after her now. And what had happened to Joey? How had he vanished? Where was he? She hoped he was in a better place than she was.

"*Emma,*" the voice like hers whispered urgently. "*Emma, listen. I haven't got much time so you have to listen. The other voice you hear, the horrible one? You mustn't listen to it. Don't believe what it says. Do you understand?*"

"You said I'd be looked after," Emma said out loud, aware she sounded like a petulant child.

"*You will be. But first, you'll have to find a way out of there.*"

"There is no way out of here," Emma snapped. "Now leave me alone."

She stuck her fingers in her ears, as if the voice was coming from someone sitting right next to her, and it sort of worked. The other Emma voice grew fainter, like a voice from another room. It pleaded with her to listen, but that was the last thing Emma wanted to do. But then the other voice came again and there was nothing she could do to block it out.

"*Emma,*" it rasped. "*Emma, listen to me.*"

Emma tried to formulate the word *NO* in her head, but it didn't work and the voice went on.

"*Do you want to get out of there? Of course you do. That cell is no place for you. You haven't done anything wrong. I can get you out, but you have to do something. You have to give yourself over completely to me.*"

***

Pete Buckler had been standing in the corridor for an hour or so, since the woman in Cell 14 had been taken away. He felt a bit foolish guarding an empty cell, but nobody had given him further orders, and until that changed, he intended to stay there on the lightest duty he'd had for a long time. He was leaning against the wall, wondering whether he should even sit down, when he suddenly heard a banging coming from the cell two doors down. He hadn't even known it was occupied, but there was certainly *someone* in there thumping on the door. Buckler pull out his phone.

"Hey, Control?" he said, unable to suppress a waver in his voice. "Is someone in Cell 16?"

"That's classified, Buckler," the controller replied.

"Yeah, well, your *classified* is banging the hell out of the cell door. I'm attending."

Before Control could argue, Buckler hung up and headed to the cell door. By the time he got there, the banging had stopped, and he paused, listening. For a moment, there was no sound at all. Then, just as he raised his hand to the lock panel, there was a loud *thump* of something hit the door hard from the inside. He jumped back in surprise.

"Jesus," he gasped, his heart pounding. He took a deep breath and reached out to operate the lock.

"Right," he said loudly, "keep the bloody noise down or—"

Before he could finish, the lock clicked, and the door opened. Something came hurtling out of the cell and hit him full force. Recovering, he was astonished to come face-to-face with a teenaged girl who had run into him so hard she'd nearly knocked him off his feet and was now trying to grab at the front of his jacket.

He tried to fend her off with one hand, while also trying to pull his sidearm from his hip holster with the other. But somehow, impossibly, the girl was too strong for him. One of her hands grabbed him by the throat, and he was pushed back against the wall on the other side of the corridor. His shoulders hit the brickwork, and he slid up the wall, his feet leaving the floor. He could barely breathe; she was crushing his larynx.

"*Don't struggle,*" the girl said, and her voice sounded like no teenage girl Buckler had ever come across, "*or I'll kill you now. Nod your head if you understand.*"

It was all Buckler could do to move at all, but he somehow managed to nod *yes.*

"*Good.*" Her voice went through him like chalk on a blackboard. "*I'm going to let you down. When I do, I want to see whoever is in charge of this hole, and I want to see them NOW!*"

Chapter Twenty-One

"We don't know what demolished Nelson's Column and killed all those people," Davina Watson said to an uncomprehending Joey Cale. "But we know what it wasn't. It wasn't a bomb. It wasn't a missile. And it certainly wasn't a gas main, as some people have speculated. Have a look at this." She tapped on her keyboard and turned her monitor to face Joey.

He looked at the grainy image of Nelson's Column on the screen and shook his head. There was something odd about the sky above the statue's head, but he couldn't make out what it was. "Is that…?" He tilted his head as if that would make a difference. "No. I have no idea what I'm looking at."

"It's the only picture that exists of the seconds before the Column detonated," Watson explained. "Sure, everyone's seen the footage of it blowing up—the news crew that caught it sent it straight over—but there are no other pictures of the time just before, or after. We don't think it's a fake but we can't be a hundred percent sure.

"Think about that for a second. Trafalgar Square. Packed with tourists and people just going about their business. Pretty much every single damn one of them would have had a phone on them. Loads would have had cameras as well. And yet this is the only real photograph that exists, and believe me, we've looked.

"Whatever flattened the Column also killed everyone's phones and wiped the memory cards of everyone's cameras. This only exists because by chance someone had been to a party the night before, and they'd given out a load of those old throwaway cameras as a joke. The story goes that the camera was found in the debris and someone got the film developed. This is a scan of the photo, which is why the quality is crap. What do you make of the sky?"

Joey squinted again at the screen, moving his head back and forward, trying to get a better view. "Don't know. There's something there, but I can't make it out. It looks almost like…a hole?"

"A hole in the sky. Impossible, isn't it? And yet there it is. If this photo is genuine, then we think something came out of that hole and hit Trafalgar Square almost like a mini-nuke. We also believe the Government have a fair idea of what it was and is covering it up. I've studied the press a great deal over the years, and I've never seen such a lack of information. In this day and age, you can find out about anything, anywhere, but the only information you can get about this incident is what the Government releases. And we are very much aware that what they release is not true."

"Do you have a theory?" Joey asked.

"We didn't. Then your friend Raj showed up, and we realised very quickly there was a hell of a lot we didn't know. There have always been theories about other worlds, but nobody has ever been able to prove it, not really. Not until somebody showed up who actually came from one. And with a dog. Quantum physics never predicted that one."

Joey laughed despite himself. Then a thought struck him. "Is there a Raj in this world? And what about Anna and the kids, Evan and Ruby? Raj said they were all here. And what about me? Is there another me?"

"One question at a time. Easiest first. Evan and Ruby are fine and in a safe house. They do also exist in this world, but with their age, we just want to leave them alone. Your Evan and Ruby are happy, well cared for and safe. At some point, we'll take you to see them, but not yet. The Green Jackets are looking for you, and the last thing we'd want to do is lead anyone to the kids."

"No," Joey agreed. "I'm just glad they're safe."

"As for the rest... There was a Raj in this world. He worked for us, but the Green Jackets got him. Your Raj saw it happen. We picked him up before we knew it wasn't *our* Raj, if you follow. Then we found out our Raj was dead, and for a while all hell let loose, especially when your Raj told us his story and we heard about you.

"We didn't quite believe it at first. Well, you wouldn't, would you? But then Anna Mallory appeared and the kids were found, and there was no way of denying it. There's still plenty we don't understand but we're getting there. Raj has slotted in perfectly here, even though I don't think he feels very comfortable with what he has to do sometimes."

"You said Anna was here, but Raj was a bit...cagey when I asked him."

Watson paused for a moment. "Anna is more of a problem. The Anna you knew is here. She said she wanted a normal life, and she joined us for a little while, but didn't want to stay. We couldn't force her, but, for reasons I'll show you in a minute, we couldn't just let her wander around, so we had her closely monitored. A little while ago, she went totally off-radar and we think she's been taken. If she has, she'll be in a holding facility near Leicester, but that really could be a problem."

Watson turned her monitor screen so she could type something into the computer. When she turned it back to Joey again, he was shocked by what he saw. It was Anna, but she looked very different: sleekly groomed, dressed in some kind of uniform, and her face had a hardness that sent a chill down his spine.

"The Anna Mallory of this world took rather a different career path to yours. She joined the police, not the NHS, and did very well. After Nelson's Column came down, she was recruited to head up the new security service. Anna Mallory is the head of the Green Jackets, Joey. That's the problem. That's why we fear for your Anna."

Joey stared at the image on the screen. This was all a bit too much to take in, and it reminded him of something he should never have forgotten.

"Emma," he said. "Emma Winrush. The one from my world…died." He found it hard even to say the word. "But the one from this world… Where is she? Have the Green Jackets got her? Raj wouldn't say."

After a moment's hesitation, Watson answered, "Yes. That is our information."

"Then we have to help her. *You* have to help her."

"We are monitoring the situation, believe me. We've been watching Miss Winrush ever since Raj arrived and told us his story. There's no indication whatsoever that Emma Winrush had done anything to interest the authorities, so we're curious as to why they've taken her. The only conclusion we can come to is that they've seen her with you and linked her to us."

"Why did they only take her? The one who came after us didn't seem interested in me at all. He only shot me because I stood up for Emma."

"We don't know, Joey. But seeing as she hasn't done anything wrong, she may well be safer with them than associating with you."

"So that's it. You're just going to leave her there?"

"Not at all. If we feel she is in the slightest danger, we will do all we can to help her. Since Raj turned up, we've been keeping a very close eye on all of you. There are deep-cover Catesby agents in all sorts of places. I don't think you need to worry about Emma. It's you we're more interested in at the moment."

This brought to the forefront of Joey's mind a question that had been gnawing at him since the conversation began.

"What about me? Is there another me here?"

Watson shook her head. "No. But there was. We trawled through the records and found that, in our world, Joey Cale died of a heart defect shortly after birth. You're unique, Joey. There is only one of you."

Chapter Twenty-Two

BILLY RADLEY WAS fuming. For a while now, he'd felt like he was being sidelined. Chowdhury seemed to prefer working with Liza Hunt these days, and Billy only ever seemed to be called on for crap driving jobs. Hunt was the one who usually got picked for any decent stuff. If he didn't know Chowdhury better, he'd have thought there was something going on there. The other Raj Chowdhury, the one who got killed, used to treat Billy better, but this one had something against him, and Billy didn't know what, which just left him confused and angry.

Billy had always given his all to the Catesbys, ever since they offered him a job to get him away from the gang trouble on the estate. Being in a crew was just something you did. Everyone did it, either through boredom, or fear or a need to belong. Billy did it mainly through fear. If you weren't in one gang, then you always had to look over your shoulder for the other crews. At least if you belonged to one, there was a degree of safety in numbers.

So he shoplifted, did some grass but tried to stay away from the worst of the violence, though that wasn't always possible, especially not on match days. He had always thought he would end up dead or in a cell, but after his last brush with the law, three days after his nineteenth birthday, he was offered the choice: do some time or do something a bit more useful. He'd seen what life inside did to you—it had happened to too many of his mates and some of his family. You ended up with either an attitude or a habit.

He'd been looking for a way out of the cycle of drinking and fighting without losing face. The guy who had come to see him in Marsh Lane Police Station had promised him a new identity, and said the crew he ran with would never be able to find him. They were true to their word, and even though Billy had stayed on Merseyside for the last twenty-odd years, he'd never heard from his old crew again.

But now, after all his loyal service, here he was, sidelined. Hunt had gone off with Chowdhury to find this Cale kid everyone was talking about. Billy had heard they were back now, but only on the grapevine. Nobody had bothered to tell him officially. So he was cooling his heels, having a smoke by the ramp to the car park and wondering why a row of half a dozen seagulls standing on the railings at the edge of the pavement were eyeing him up like he was a bag of chips.

The burned man seemingly came out of nowhere. One minute, the street was empty, the next, Billy's nostrils were assaulted by a smell like an overdone barbecue. He looked to see where the smell had come from and saw what looked like a survivor of a war zone crawling towards him along the pavement. The man—or at least, Billy assumed it was a man—was clearly in a great deal of pain. His clothes were in shreds, and smoke was coming off them and what might have been long hair. Billy gagged at the smell and hesitantly moved toward the man, keeping one hand on his phone in case he needed to call for backup, but the wreck of a human in front of him didn't look like a threat. He didn't look like he was going to be alive much longer.

"You okay, mate?" Billy asked, though the answer was pretty obvious.

"Help me," the man gasped, reaching out a hand. Billy noticed the skin on the hand and arm was scorched and blistered.

"I'll get an ambulance," Billy said, taking his phone out.

"N-no," came the hoarse reply. "Need to…get inside." As he said this, the burned man tried to stand but fell back onto the pavement.

Billy rushed forward to help him. "Only place you're going is hospital, mate." He crouched beside him, trying not to breathe in the smoke still rising from the man's hair and the tatters of cloth which barely covered him. The man got to his knees but still couldn't manage to get to stand.

"Need…to…find…" he managed to get out before collapsing into a fit of coughing.

"Easy," Billy said. "What is it you need?"

With a strength Billy really wasn't expecting from him, the man pushed him in the chest. Caught by surprise, Billy fell over backwards.

The man finally pulled himself upright and staggered towards the warehouse. Billy scrambled to his feet and caught up with him as he reached the entrance. He got a hand on the man's shoulder and had to swallow back the bile which rose to his throat at the blisters oozing under his hand. The man wrestled against Billy's grip and nearly got free, but then his strength evaporated and he collapsed against a wall.

"All right, mate," Billy said. "Take it easy. You can't go in there."

"Have to," the man replied, his voice little more than a croak. "Have to…find…Joey Cale."

"*What did you say?* Who the hell are you anyway?"

The man turned his head then and looked at Billy. Beneath the leaking, blackened skin of his eyelids, his eyes suddenly flashed a fiery red and he said a name. As soon as he said it, Billy grabbed his phone out of his pocket and hit the first number on his speed dial.

"It's Radley," he said when his call was answered. "I'm at the entrance. I need Raj Chowdhury down here *now*! … No, it's got to be Raj. … Because I need a frigging doctor, that's why. I've got a badly injured man. … No, I can't call an ambulance. This guy's just used one of the hot codes. … Yes, that's what I said. Tell Raj I need him right now, because I've got a guy here who looks like he's about to peg out any minute. He says his name is Remick."

Chapter Twenty-Three

RICHARD WELLS FOUND it quite unnerving, sitting on the viewing side of the one-way glass looking into the small interview room. A short flight and a quick drive had brought them here, but Wells still had no real idea why. Martin Buxton had been evasive, just said there was something he wanted Wells to see. What that might be was clearly important enough for the two of them and Carla Lockhart to be pulled away from their investigations.

Buxton sat opposite the woman in the room, Lockhart in a chair to one side; they had agreed Wells would observe from the outside. Too many people in the room might be intimidating, and they needed the woman's cooperation.

It was the woman Wells found most troubling. Her face was so familiar, yet somehow...not. Everyone knew the face of Anna Mallory—it was on the news so often—yet this woman who bore her face looked somehow smaller, like Mallory's twin who had fallen on hard times.

Voices from the room came over a loudspeaker next to the window.

"As I said, Anna," Buxton was saying, "we mean you no harm or distress. It's your help we need more than anything."

"I told you, I don't know if I can," the woman replied, not meeting Buxton's eyes.

"Don't be so modest. We're aware of your remarkable abilities."

"I don't know what you mean."

"I think you do, and I can only apologise for the unacceptable treatment you have received at the hands of some of our guards. Let me assure you, they have been severely reprimanded, but—"

"Reprimanded. Right."

"—*but* what we are most interested in is the manner in which you have dealt with it yourself."

"I don't know what you mean," the woman repeated.

"You do, Anna. You know very well what I mean. We're fully aware you healed yourself. What we need to know is whether that's the limit of your abilities or if you can also heal others."

The woman laughed, and Wells, even listening from outside could tell it was a laugh with no humour.

"No-one can do that," she said. "Don't be ridiculous."

"It's all in your file." Buxton indicated a folder on the table. "That's why we had a doctor check you over before you came in here. You've received rough treatment from some of our staff, but you have absolutely no signs of physical injury. None at all. Now, either you have a very hardy constitution—and I have to say, you don't really look like it—or there's something else going on here."

"I'm stronger than I seem," the woman answered.

"No, you're not. In this day and age, information is key. It keeps our country and our democracy safe from those who would destroy it. We have information. We know all about you. We know you appeared from nowhere. We know you had contact with the anarchists who call themselves the Catesby Foundation. We know that you, and several others came from—shall we say—somewhere else? And we know you have the ability to heal.

"So no more games, Ms. Mallory. We know what you can do. We just need to see it in action. If you cooperate, you will be out of your cell rather sooner than expected. But you *will* cooperate."

Through the window, Wells watched as Buxton got up and opened the door. A uniformed officer came in, his hand heavily bandaged. Dark patches of blood seeped through the dressing.

"Mr. Lawrence here has had an unfortunate accident," Buxton said. "It's a nasty cut, but rather than take him to A and E, we thought you might like to help."

"I can't," the woman replied flatly. "Get him to a hospital."

"You don't seem to understand your situation. Do you like your cell, Anna? Do you want to stay in it for a long time?"

"You can't do that. There are rules."

"You're being held here under the Prevention of Terrorism Act. The normal rules don't apply. We can hold you for as long as we see fit. *Or* you can help us and we'll see about making those charges go away. Your choice."

There was a long silence in the room.

"All right," she said. "Let me see that hand."

Wells leaned forward, getting as close to the window as he could.

Buxton unwound the bandage from the officer's hand. Even from a distance, Wells could see it was a serious injury, extending from the web between the officer's thumb and forefinger across the back of his hand. It was a neat cut, though, as if it had been inflicted with precision. Neat but deep. Wells observed the woman lay her hand on the officer's, blood trickling out from between her fingers.

"Is it working?" Buxton asked eagerly.

"Wait! I need to concentrate. I can't just..." She gasped and stiffened slightly.

From where he was, Wells couldn't clearly see what was happening, but he saw the confusion on the officer's face and the keen, almost greedy look on Buxton's.

After a minute or so, the woman moved away, and Buxton cleaned the officer's hand with a surgical wipe he'd produced from somewhere—Wells had been too caught up in the action to notice. Where the open wound had been, there was barely a mark. Wells was astounded. He was getting used to seeing remarkable things these days, but he had never seen anything quite like this.

"Is that it?" the woman asked. "Can I go now?"

Buxton sat back in his chair. "Thank you, Mr. Lawrence." He gestured for the officer to leave the room. He waited for the man to go before he addressed the woman again. "That was impressive. Very impressive, and confirms you're the right person for the job."

"Job?" the woman asked. "What job? I thought you said—"

"We needed your help, yes. That was only the start of it—a test to see if you had the ability we thought you did. What comes next is far more important."

It was then that Wells began to understand why they were testing this woman, and why Carla Lockhart had been sitting there, silently observing, all this time. They wanted to know if this woman, this duplicate Anna Mallory, could actually heal the dead.

Chapter Twenty-Four

ELSEWHERE IN THE same building, another Anna Mallory was about to have a rather different kind of interview, and she wasn't at all happy about it. She had been summoned because a teenage girl had insisted on speaking to her. The girl—who had been brought here simply so the Catesbys couldn't get to her first and had, up until now, shown absolutely no signs of violence or aggression—had hospitalised and nearly killed a guard with her bare hands. She'd threatened that unless she got to see Mallory in person, she would walk out of the place, damaging anyone who got in her way.

Once she'd been told Mallory was on her way, she calmly returned to her cell and waited, the guards hovering around outside with no idea what to do. Even Jordan Levez, the most senior officer in the facility, seemed bewildered and confused, and he was not a man to flap under any circumstances, which was why he was there.

"There are no precedents for this," he said when Mallory arrived. "Anyone else, we would have taken them down."

"I'm sure you did all you could against such a severe threat," Mallory retorted.

"You didn't see what she did to Buckler. She nearly broke his neck. We have CCTV footage—"

"She's a seventeen-year-old girl, Levez. When Buckler gets out of hospital, I want him sacked. Now, tell me again exactly what this savage teenager said."

"Just that she wanted to speak to the most senior person, or she would leave. That person was clearly not me."

"I'm not surprised. She could see your fear, Levez. I can see it too, and I don't like it."

"And then there's her voice..."

"Her voice?"

"Wait till you hear it. It's not the voice of a teenage girl. It's... it's like nothing I've ever heard."

"Take me to see her," Mallory ordered. "Then you go and have a nice lie down."

Normally a prisoner who made such threats would be rapidly neutralised—with extreme sanction if necessary. But not this one. This one was not to be harmed under any circumstances. Mallory wasn't used to being ordered around—certainly not by teenage girls—and she was furious about it. But then she met the girl face-to-face and realised: Emma Winrush was no ordinary girl.

"*Anna Mallory. I suppose you'll do.*"

"I'll have to do," Mallory replied, drawing up to her full height, which was a good two inches taller than the purple-haired girl in front of her. "You won't get higher than me."

"*We both know that is not true.*" The girl gave a rasping laugh. "*But for now, I will speak to you. You can convey what I tell you to your superiors.*"

"I'll decide that, Miss Winrush," Mallory said. She was beginning to think she might have treated Levez a bit harshly. Winrush was certainly nothing like any teenager Mallory had met before. Considering she was still at school and had no record at all, she was icy calm, and Mallory didn't like that. And that voice...*Jesus*, Levez was right about that.

"Now, what is it you want?" Mallory tried to sound firm and authoritative, a role she always played well, but behind it, her brain was asking just one question over and over: *where is that voice coming from?* Even the words it was using didn't sound like they should come from a seventeen-year-old girl.

"*I don't have much time, so you need to listen. I don't have the strength to appear to you in person yet, although I'm getting stronger. In the meantime, I must use this pathetic vessel. There are some things you must know. One is that the thing which has been found must* not *be disturbed. Do you know what I mean by that?"*

"I can't give out classified information," Mallory answered—a stock response to cover her shock at what she had heard. How in God's name did Winrush know about the body? It had only just been found and only a handful of people knew about it. "Where do you get your information?" she demanded. "Someone will lose their job for this. At best."

"*That is—what did you call it?—classified.*" The girl laughed again, then grew more serious. "*Do not disturb it. It must be kept intact at all costs. You risk catastrophe on a scale you cannot possibly imagine otherwise. Do you understand?*"

"I hear what you say, but I'll need a bit more to go on than that. I can't do anything on the say-so of a kid like you."

"*I am hardly a child, Anna Mallory. I am older than your brain can calculate. But have it your way. You can either act on what I say or risk the consequences. It is your choice. Now, the next thing you must do is to bring the Cale boy in. He cannot be allowed to roam free. Do you understand?*"

"I understand you want to see your boyfriend, but again, I'm not going to do it on your say-so." Mallory absolutely was not going to mention that the order had already been given to bring Joey Cale in and that it had come from higher up the chain of command. "Anything else?"

"*Just this. I know your opponents have found a man called Remick. He is weak and injured at present but will be extremely dangerous when he recovers. That must not happen. You must find him and stop him.*"

"Stop him? Stop him from doing what? And stop him how?"

"*By killing him. How else?*"

"Okay, I've heard enough. The stupid voice doesn't scare me, and I'm not stopping an operation like this, or having someone terminated because some goth kid tells me to."

Mallory was expecting some response from Emma Winrush—fury maybe—but instead was surprised when the girl sagged visibly and dropped to her knees.

"Winrush?" Mallory asked.

"I'm...I'm okay," was the reply, and the voice was what Mallory would have expected from a girl that age. She looked up with fearful eyes. "Wh-what happened? Where am I?"

"Don't try that with me," Mallory said, grabbing the girl's arm. "On your feet." Emma Winrush didn't fight her. "I don't know what your game is, girl, but you've picked the wrong day to mess with me. Now I'm going to have you put somewhere you'll never get out of, and you'll be staying there until we decide how you're going to answer for putting one of my staff in hospital."

Mallory dragged Emma back to the cell and pushed her roughly inside, slamming the door after her. Then she pulled out her phone, keyed in a number and spoke into it.

"It's Mallory," she said. "All under control here. But I want this girl transported out of here to a secure unit ASAP. And I want the key thrown away."

* * *

From inside the cell, Emma heard those words, and then heard Mallory's footsteps recede down the corridor. Only then did she allow herself to smile.

Chapter Twenty-Five

DIED," JOEY SAID. "I died."

"Well, not you," Davina Watson replied. "The Joey Cale of our world. He died a week after birth from a congenital heart defect. Poor kid had no chance from the sound of it."

"I did. I had a chance. I survived."

"It's a funny thing. There are so many similarities between you guys and the versions of you in this world. But there are differences too. Some of the differences are small, some are much bigger. Look at Anna Mallory. One version is a nurse, the other is the head of the security service. The Evan and Ruby of this world are happy kids. Their parents are together and all is fine. Yet the ones who came here with you had an abusive stepfather, from what they have told the counsellor who's working with them. The two versions of Raj seem pretty much the same except the Raj on this world is now dead. Why the differences? We're not sure. Maybe it's an environment thing. They're different because this world is different."

"It certainly is," Joey said, without irony.

Watson continued as if he hadn't spoken at all. "We've worked with Raj, mapping out timelines, and here's the weird thing. Everything in our history is pretty much the same as yours—kings, queens, world events—the lot. But we think we've identified the exact date when the two timelines diverged."

"What? How? How did you manage to do that?"

"Probably because we were looking for it. It was Raj's idea, actually. He suggested it almost as a joke, but when we looked, it fitted. The date is September 27th 1999. Which is—"

"A week after my birthday. I know." Joey sat back in his chair and stared at Watson. "Come off it. It's a coincidence, surely."

"That's what we thought. In this world, the 27th of September 1999 has another, deeper significance, though. The day baby Joey Cale sadly died, was also the day Tony Blair resigned."

"Resigned?" Joey was stunned. "No, he didn't."

"He did here, because of a massive financial scandal. It came out of nowhere and spread like wildfire. Blair wasn't directly implicated, but it happened on his watch. It was one of the most shocking incidents in modern political history and it changed the country and the world. He wasn't succeeded by Gordon Brown as everyone expected, but by a backbencher called Ian Glover who virtually nobody had heard of.

"Glover bowed to pressure from the right-wing press and called a snap general election. Labour lost with nearly as big a landslide as they'd won the previous one. But the scandal hit every party to one extent or another, and the election was won by a new party formed by some of the wealthiest people in the country. They called it the New Morality Party and promised a hard line on crime and corruption, and MPs who saw which way the wind was blowing defected to it in a hurry.

"The Labour Party went into complete meltdown and hasn't been anywhere near Government since. They aren't even the biggest opposition party.

"So there you go. Coincidence or not, the timeline of your world and the timeline of ours split in a massive way the day Joey Cale died here but didn't die in your world."

"I can't take this in," Joey said. "Sorry. It's just not—"

He was interrupted by a knock at the door. Watson pressed a button on her desk, and the door clicked open. It was Raj, carrying two mugs of coffee and a couple of cellophane-wrapped sandwiches.

"Sorry," he said. "Just needed to give Misha a quick walk."

"Don't worry," Watson said. "I've been filling Joey in on a few things. I think I've blown his mind, though, so if it's all right with you, I'll skip the coffee. It might be best if you show Joey to his quarters. He could probably do with a rest and a bit of time to think. He can have something to eat there."

"No problem." Raj left the drinks on Watson's desk. "Come on, Joey. I'll show you what facilities the Catesby Hotel has to offer."

Joey followed Raj out of Watson's office and down the corridor.

"I know," Raj said as they walked. "It's all a bit too much to take in, isn't it?"

"I can't," Joey agreed. "It's just…I don't know."

"Yeah. Who'd have thought Mariah Carey would marry Brad Pitt? It's certainly a different world."

Joey laughed at this despite himself. Raj could always do that. They walked on down a couple more corridors and stopped outside a door.

"Here we go. The key code is your date of birth reversed. We'll change it to something less guessable later. I'm next door, by the way. You'll have to drop in later and see Misha. Don't forget your butties." He handed the sandwiches over. "Oh, hang on…" He dug about in his inside jacket pocket and pulled out his still-buzzing phone. "Sorry. I'll just get this.

"Yes, Liza. What is it? … What? Slow down. He said what? … Okay. I'll be right there." He hung up and looked at Joey, all good humour gone from his face. "Make yourself at home, Joey. I've got to, er…deal with something. Please don't leave your quarters. I'll be back soon, but I might need you."

Joey nodded agreement as Raj hurried off and then used the key code as instructed, entering a small, plain, utilitarian room. There was a single bed along one wall; he sat on it and ate the first half of his sandwich, but before he could eat the other half, he was overcome by a wave of sadness and homesickness.

He lay there for nearly half an hour waiting for it to pass, and when it didn't, he knew what he had to do. He left the room and cautiously made his way along the corridor, remembering the way they had come until he found the lift, which he took down to the car park and the road that led back into the city centre.

From there, he caught a train and walked the short distance from the station to the street where, in another world, he had lived all his life. Everything Watson had told him had unnerved and confused him, and he needed to grab hold of something halfway familiar. Except when he got there, it wasn't familiar at all. He remembered his friend Sam—who would never have met Joey Cale in this world—telling him that after his family moved house when he was young, his dad sometimes used to go back to the old house and just sit in his car outside, looking at what the new occupants had done to the place. Joey felt like that now.

When he had visited this house before, thinking it was his own, he hadn't really looked at it properly. Now, he could see the window frames were wood-look uPVC, not the rather tatty brown-painted wooden ones he was used to. The curtains were different—even the gate was a different colour, dark green not black. It wasn't his home anymore. Never had been, never would be.

In his parents' house—his home—there was a picture of a van Joey had drawn on the wall the first time they decorated. He must have been about three at the time, and it wasn't a very good van, but it was still recognisable. It had been papered over several times since, and every time the old wallpaper was stripped away, there was Joey's van. It would not exist in this house because Joey had never existed here. He felt a strong pang of sadness for the Joey Cale who had died seventeen years ago.

With a heavy heart, he turned to head back to the station, planning to get a train to somewhere, anywhere. Ideally, he wanted to find and free Emma, since Watson and her crew didn't want to. He couldn't fail her again. As for everything else—this wasn't his world, and their problems were not his problems. He didn't belong here and didn't want to get involved. That, in turn, raised more questions. Was there any escape? Was there any chance at all of ever getting back home to his own world? Or was he stuck here forever? He didn't even know where to begin with any of it.

He was so preoccupied he didn't notice the black Audi on the other side of the road. He didn't see it move as soon as he did. He didn't see its two green-coated occupants until it was too late.

***

Because of all the fuss caused by Remick's sudden and unexpected arrival at the Catesby Foundation HQ, nobody realised Joey had gone until an hour later.

Chapter Twenty-Six

RAJ RELUCTANTLY LEFT Joey to his own devices and raced down to the entrance of the warehouse. There, he found Billy Radley pacing backwards and forwards impatiently. Nearby was the form of a man, curled up in a foetal position against the wall, tendrils of smoke still drifting from his clothes.

"He's in a really bad way," Radley said when Raj arrived. "I was going to call an ambulance, but then he used one of the hot codes. Who is he, Raj?"

"An old friend." Raj crouched down beside the man. "If it's really him. Thanks. I'll take it from here."

"D'you need a hand getting him inside?"

"It's fine, Billy. I'll take care of it. Take a walk and get some air. You look like you could do with it."

Raj waited until Radley had walked away, then leaned in closer to examine the wreck of a man beside him. From what Raj could see of the head and body where the cloth had burned away, there didn't seem to be an inch of skin that wasn't raw and blistered. He looked like he'd been hit by napalm. Even so, his face was familiar, though Raj had only seen it once, and quite some time ago.

"Remick. What the hell happened to you?"

With some difficulty, Remick turned his head. "Raj." Even his voice sounded like pain. "You came."

"Of course I did. As soon as I heard it was you. Listen, we need to get you to hospital." Raj went for his pocket and his phone, but Remick reached out a surprisingly strong hand and grabbed his wrist.

"No!" he gasped and started coughing. Raj helped him sit up a little, worrying he might choke. Once the coughing subsided, Remick spoke again, but this time his voice was so weak Raj had to lean in close to hear him. "No hospital. They won't...they won't have seen anything like me. Get me...inside."

"We can't treat you here!" Raj protested. "We don't have the facilities. You'll die!"

"No," Remick croaked. "I'll heal with time. But get me inside. There are things you need...to know. Help me up."

"This isn't wise, Remick. I'm a doctor. I know about these things."

"Just help me, Raj."

Raj was going to argue again, but there was something about Remick's insistent tone that stopped him. Against his better judgement, he hooked an arm around Remick's back and under his armpit, and pulled him upright. An unnatural heat radiated from Remick's body.

"Now think of your room," Remick instructed, his voice barely more than a whisper.

"Oh, no," Raj said. "No way. There's too much furniture in there. And a dog. It's too dangerous."

"Have a little faith."

"Faith?" Raj laughed humourlessly. "In a demon. Yeah, why not?"

He concentrated, visualising his room and homing in on the clear space in the middle of the floor occupied only by a brown fleece rug. He just hoped Misha wasn't sleeping on it as she sometimes did. He focused on the rug, on feeling it under his feet and then...

...the rug was there. He gulped back the nausea that always accompanied his travelling, relieved to see Remick was still with him and in apparently no worse a state than he was before. Misha, startled by Raj's sudden appearance, gave a gruff bark and padded over to see him.

"Just a minute, Misha." Raj guided Remick over to the bed and lay him down. "I'll get you some water. Nothing stronger though."

Remick tried to laugh, but it came out as a cough. "Couldn't... handle it. Water would be good."

Raj went into the small en-suite bathroom and turned on the tap, letting the water run for a moment so it was as cold as possible, and then filled a glass he kept by the sink. He took it back to the room, where at first it seemed Remick had fallen asleep, but he'd only closed his eyes and opened them as Raj approached. Raj helped him sit up slightly and held the glass to his cracked lips. Remick took a sip, spluttered, then took another sip. Swallowing with difficulty, he waved the glass away.

"You need to rest now," Raj said.

"In a minute. I need to talk to you first. I need to warn you."

"Warn me about what? What happened to you, Remick?"

"Saunders."

At the mention of that name, Raj's blood ran cold.

"The being who calls himself Saunders. After he went through the portal, I went after him. Got out just before the world collapsed."

"How could you go after him? You weren't there."

"I think you forget sometimes what I am, Raj." Remick stopped speaking to cough. Raj offered him more water, but he shook his head. "I saw Joey when I first got here. I think he saw me too, but I'm not sure. Then I went looking for Saunders. He wasn't here yet. He was somewhere...between. I tried to stop him getting to this world, but..."

"He beat you?"

"We both lost. He left me there and fled. I believe his arrival here didn't go unnoticed." Remick's head sank back onto the pillow. It was all he could do to keep his eyes open, but Raj's interest was piqued now. Remick could sleep all he wanted soon, but first Raj needed answers.

"It was Trafalgar Square, wasn't it?" he asked. "That's what you mean."

"Bad…landing…"

"Is he still there?" Raj got no reply so asked again. "Remick, is Saunders still under Trafalgar Square?"

Remick muttered something that might have been 'somewhere else' but lapsed into sleep, and Raj didn't have the heart to wake him. If Anna had been here, she might have been able to do something, even if she just sped up the healing process a bit. But until Anna was found—and presumably freed—it was down to Raj, though in all his years of studying, the medical care of demons had somehow never come up.

Moving a chair to the side of the bed, Raj sat, and Misha joined him, resting her large head on his knee. He put his hand on her head, and together they waited.

Chapter Twenty-Seven

BILLY RADLEY WAS fuming. Again. He was the one who'd found the burning man. He was the one who'd recognised the hot code for what it was and called Chowdhury down. But had he been given any credit for it? Had he shite. He'd been sent off to have a *nice little walk*, while Chowdhury muscled in yet again.

In truth, Billy was quite glad for a reason to walk away. It prevented him from punching Chowdhury in his smug face. He crossed the road and climbed through a gap in the fence of the scrap-metal yard opposite. It was private property, but he often came through here, and no-one ever tried to stop him. On the other side of the rusting piles of scrap was the waterfront, and he liked to look out across the Mersey, watching the ships or, on clear days, gazing across to the Wirral.

He reached the waterfront and lit up a cigarette, inhaling deeply and already feeling a little calmer. A line of red from the setting sun broke up the grey of the horizon, but dusk was beginning to settle in. Sometimes, when it was really clear, you could see the hills of Wales beyond. There was a standing joke in Liverpool that if you could see the Welsh hills, it was going to rain. If you couldn't see them, it was already raining. Billy didn't much care whether it was raining or not. He just liked being in the fresh air. It made his cigarettes taste better.

It was then that he noticed the gulls. Just like earlier, there was a row of them, this time along the edge of the quay, six or seven, all craning their white necks and fixing Billy with their angry-looking yellow eyes. Billy stared back, but if this was a staring match, he knew he would lose; gulls didn't seem to blink, they just stared.

"I don't know what you're looking at," Billy said out loud, flicking his cigarette end into the water. "I haven't got any scran for you."

The bird closest to Billy watched the dog-end's progress in the river, then swivelled its head back and carried on regarding Billy. The gesture seemed rather un-birdlike, and Billy found it disturbing, like there was something going on behind the bird's eyes—some intelligence, some thought process of which he'd always assumed birds were not capable.

The rational part of his brain told him it was stupid to be so bothered by a bird, and he turned his back on it and walked a few yards along the quayside. It wasn't that he was scared of the thing; after all he'd been through in his life, it would take more than some dumb seagull to scare Billy Radley. He just didn't like being watched and certainly not by *those* eyes.

His irritation at the gull brought back the feelings he'd been trying to escape by coming here, and he decided, there and then: *Sod Chowdhury, I'm going straight to the top.* On his next break, he'd go and see Watson, tell her he was fed up being kept on the sidelines and demand something more interesting to do. Of course, Watson thought the world of Chowdhury, for some reason, and wouldn't hear a word said against him, but Billy would make her see sense. He'd served the Foundation so well and for so long, she must surely be able to see his worth, and if she didn't, he'd stay in her face until she did. If that didn't work, he was prepared to walk away.

One more quick cigarette and he would head back and see her.

He'd just opened the pack when he heard a fluttering overhead, and a shadow passed over him. Then that damn seagull landed right in front of him. Before he could react, its half dozen mates had joined it, forming a rough line that blocked his path.

"What the...?" he began and turned away from the birds, ready to go back the way he'd come, but more of the little bastards had landed behind him, cutting off his escape route. He clapped his hands together, hoping to startle them. When that didn't work, he clapped again and swore loudly at the birds. They just stood there, staring at him. Looking around on the ground, he spotted a discarded lager bottle. He picked it up and hurled it at the quayside near the gulls. The smash of the shattering glass echoed off the stone, and two of the gulls leapt up, beating their wings. One flew a short distance and landed again; the other stayed in the air above Billy's head. Then it attacked.

The assault was so sudden Billy barely had time to raise his arms to protect himself as the bird came straight at his face. He lashed out and caught the gull with a solid backhand to its chest. The gull gave out a loud caw and retreated a little before it lunged for another attack. This time, its beak caught Billy with a glancing blow to his forehead. Billy felt pain and the wetness where it had drawn blood, but he ignored it and started to run.

The gull swooped after him as he ran headlong into the scrapyard. Spotting a broken plank of wood on the ground, he grabbed it, swinging it around. It connected with the gull in a flurry of feathers. With a dull, wet thump, the bird hit the ground, flapped once and lay still. Billy stood over it and kept hitting it with the plank until he was absolutely sure it was dead. A black puddle of blood leaked from its beak, but even in death its yellow eyes were staring.

Breathing hard, Billy mopped some of the blood from his forehead with his sleeve. The wound stung, and he was starting with the mother of all headaches—nothing some paracetamol wouldn't sort out when he got back to the warehouse. He'd have to see if he could clean up the cut as well, and come up with a story if anyone noticed. He really didn't want to have to explain he had acquired the cut in a heroic battle with a psychopathic seagull.

It was as he set off across the scrapyard, heading back to the warehouse, that he heard the voice.

"*Billy*," it said.

He stopped walking and looked around. Some of the guys who worked in the scrapyard were so used to seeing him they greeted him when he passed, but he didn't think any of them knew his name, and there was no-one around—unless they were hiding in one of the wrecked, rusty cars. But no, they'd have well gone home for their tea by now. Not everyone had to live in the place they worked, like he did.

Then he heard it again, and the cut on his forehead throbbed in concert with the syllables of his name.

"*Billy.*"

"Who's there?" he demanded, a rare tremor in his voice.

"*I am in you,*" the voice said. "*I was in the bird, and now I am in the bacteria in your blood.*"

Billy stopped walking. The crack on the head he got from that bloody gull must have been harder than he thought.

"*I can help you,*" the voice said.

"Help me? Help me with what?"

"*You have been overlooked for too long. It is time you were recognised.*"

"Damn right it is," Billy replied, forgetting for a moment he was talking to a voice in his head.

"*You are worth ten of Rajeev Chowdhury. If you let me, I can help you bring him down. I can help you get the recognition you deserve.*"

"Help me? How can you help me? I can't even see you!"

"*Give yourself over to me,*" the voice said. "*I can help you make sure no-one will ever forget your name.*"

That was all it took. In that instant, Billy Radley was lost and so was the world.

PART TWO

Chapter One

PATRICE BARKER STOOD by the kitchen sink, drying the lunch dishes and watching the children play in the garden. When they had first arrived in her care, they had been quiet and withdrawn, especially Ruby. Patrice had been told a little of their background—that they came from a home with an abusive stepfather, had lived rough for a while and been through some other things not specified in their files, which she found frustrating. To give the children the right care, she needed information, but as was sometimes the case, bits of the children's past were classified, so Patrice had to listen to them and try to work it out herself.

Ruby had clearly fallen under the influence of some man, whom Evan referred to in whispers as 'Mr. Saunders'. Both children were scared of Mr. Saunders and worried he would find them. Ruby still had nightmares and on a couple of occasions had wet the bed.

Dig as she might, Patrice could find nothing about a man called Saunders or anything like it in the files, and when she'd asked Dr. Franklin, her supervisor, about it, she'd been hit by the word *classified* yet again. When Dr. Franklin came to talk to the children, it was all done privately and confidentially, and Patrice really had no idea what they discussed. All she could do was give Evan and Ruby the best home and the best care she could and hope the bad dreams would wash away with a bit of love.

In the meantime, the children were doing well at school. Ruby was very good at maths, and Evan showed an aptitude for art, although his teacher had called his paintings 'dark'. Patrice had been shown some of these paintings, and it was true that, for a boy of his age, Evan had a tendency to paint rather moody landscapes, often featuring a large hill. When Patrice asked if it was somewhere Evan had been, he had said, "Once," but elaborated no further. Patrice thought it might have been a very bad holiday, but then why would he want to keep painting it?

She watched the children running around, just two normal kids having fun. Her son Alex, who was a couple of years older than Evan, sat on a garden chair nearby reading a book, too cool to join in with the boisterous game. In a minute, she would call them all in for their lunch, but there was no hurry. Ruby and Evan were getting fresh air and exercise, and at least they weren't playing hide-and-seek. The last time they did that, Evan had successfully hidden for half an hour. Ruby had been in tears because she couldn't find him, and even Patrice had become worried when he didn't appear to be anywhere in the house. She was on the point of putting out an alert, but then Evan just turned up. When she asked where he'd been hiding, he smiled and said it was a secret. Despite her worries, Patrice was smiling too. It was very difficult to stay cross with those two.

Alex had taken to them more than some of the other children who had passed through Patrice's care. For all his bluster, he was a sensitive boy, and because he'd been bullied at school for the colour of his skin and for wanting to work hard and learn, he found it hard to trust other children. But he had become very protective of Evan and Ruby in a short space of time, and Patrice was delighted by the bond which had developed between the three children.

The only thing that really bothered her was the children's fixation with 'Joey and Emma'. They kept asking when Joey was coming to see them and talked about Emma with sadness; clearly something had happened to her. But when Patrice asked who Joey and Emma were, the kids wouldn't say, and again, Dr. Franklin had dismissed the names as classified. Another brick wall. Patrice had argued she needed to tell the children *something* because they kept asking, and eventually Dr. Franklin had conceded there was a possibility they'd get to see Joey soon, but not to tell them anything in case it didn't happen and they were disappointed. Patrice had so few details, someone could show up any time and say they were called Joey, and she'd never know if it was the right person. It was an uncertainty she found unsettling.

The constant secrecy was one of the things she hated about working for the Catesby Foundation. There were many good things about working for the Catesbys. Patrice had worked in child welfare a long time; she'd seen parents having to go to food banks to feed their children while the one guaranteed source of food, a free school dinner, was removed to cut costs. She'd seen the damage done to families by the stress of constant scrutiny by the state and was grateful there was an organisation working to challenge such injustices. But the lack of information about some of her young charges, especially Evan and Ruby, was incredibly frustrating. She worked hard to help them but knew all that work could easily be undone if they had to be moved on at a moment's notice. She worried what would happen to them if that occurred, and also how Alex would take it.

For now, though, the children played in the garden, apparently without a care in the world. Patrice finished drying the dishes, but carried on watching the children's game. She paid no attention at all to the row of starlings which had gathered on the roof of the house next door and were silently watching too.

Chapter Two

Emma Winrush sat in her cell and smiled a secret smile, as she had done off and on since the woman wearing Anna's face had dragged her in here. She had even been able to sleep since then; it had been fitful, uncomfortable and plagued by strange dreams she could no longer remember, but it was sleep all the same. She had woken early and spent some time getting used to being back in a body. Her watch told her it was nearly eight the next morning and nobody had been near her, despite the order to move her somewhere else. All she had to do was wait for it to happen; it would be her best opportunity for escape, but she was in no hurry. She had all the time in the world, and she was taking the opportunity to get used to this mind and this body. She was glad to be alive. People used that expression lightly, but Emma knew you had to die to appreciate what it *really* meant.

Becoming accustomed to the body wasn't really a problem, since it was virtually the same as the one she had left. It carried a little more weight than hers, but then it didn't belong to someone who had been living on their own for months. It also felt healthier than Emma had been used to, probably for the same reason, and because it didn't smoke. Emma found this quite confusing at first. Her mind told her she hadn't had a cigarette for a long time, but her body didn't really want one.

Then there were the scars. Emma's old body had track marks where she had cut herself, criss-crossing the arms, but this one only had one or two, and they looked quite recent. At present, she could only see them, not feel them, which was also unusual.

In the strange world in which she'd died, the scars had itched to warn her of impending danger, and she wondered if the lack of scars and subsequent lack of itching meant this body didn't possess the power. If that were the case, she would have to watch out for danger in a rather more traditional way.

So the body was different, but it was the mind Emma was finding hardest to bond with. Ever since she had somehow been ripped from her dying body, she had existed as a nothing, hardly feeling, hardly thinking. The trauma and pain of her death had virtually closed her mind down. Then there had been a brief, weird tug and a spark, and she had been dragged from one world to another. With no body, she was there, but not there.

There was, however, through the whole of this semi-existence, one constant. It was a rhythm, a beat, always there, always just ahead and out of reach. It had been there from the moment Joey Cale had picked up her corpse, kissed her and tried to bring her home. Emma Winrush's mind had followed Joey Cale's heartbeat, and it had led her to the Emma Winrush of this world. All Joey had to do was say the name 'Emma', and there she was, lodged in a head that was familiar and alien at the same time.

For a day or two, she had tried to make contact with the other Emma, but she was shouting into the void. She couldn't really blame her other self for not understanding what was happening. If the circumstances were reversed, she doubted she would have been able to comprehend it either. It was only when a third presence appeared in the mind of the Emma of this world that she had been able to gain a foothold.

She'd felt pure horror as the creature that had murdered her suddenly showed up in this mind. Saunders had been in the squirrel, and when it bit Emma, he transferred himself into her mind through the infection. But, while Saunders was occupying the thoughts of the living Emma, the dead Emma's occupancy grew stronger. She'd put the thought into the living Emma's head to try and get rid of the infection by sucking on the wound and spitting it out. She'd seen someone do it with snake venom on one of those survival programmes on TV, and it seemed to loosen Saunders' grip. It also left a mess of spittle in the corner that occasionally moved and whispered threats.

When Saunders finally fled, the minds of the two Emmas had merged, creating a mind that was somehow both of them yet also something completely new. Emma Winrush now had two sets of memories, similar in some ways, different in others, and she was no longer sure which memory belonged to which Emma, but it really didn't matter anymore. They were all hers.

She had two personalities, which, again, were nearly the same, but not quite. When both Emmas agreed, it was just like hearing an echo of her thoughts. When they differed, it was literally like being in two minds about something. It would take some getting used to, but the main thing was this new Emma Winrush had knowledge and experience of both this world and the other. That was potent combination, and one which Saunders might well know nothing about. Emma couldn't wait to meet up with Joey again and tell him. However, to do that, she had to get out of here. All she had to do was wait.

She didn't have to wait long. Apparently, when the Anna of this world gave an order, people jumped. It made Emma wonder what had happened to her. The Anna she knew had been a nurse and lacked self-confidence, but this one… What Emma picked up from her other self's memories was a country ruled by the fear of constant surveillance, so it didn't surprise her that it made some people harder, but the difference in Anna was extreme. But just at the moment, it suited Emma's purposes.

Finally, she heard footsteps outside the door. She stood and readied herself. There would probably only be one chance at this, and it absolutely had to count.

The door opened, revealing two guards and a figure in a distinctive green coat.

"Stay there," the Green Jacket ordered. Emma did as she was told.

The two guards stepped into the cell. One pulled Emma's arms behind her back, while the other fastened her wrists together with what felt like cable ties. The Green Jacket took a step closer to Emma, his face so close she could smell cigarette and alcohol breath.

"I heard what you did," he said. "Don't be getting ideas."

Emma obediently shook her head and, with a guard on either side, followed the Green Jacket out of the cell. As they walked down the corridor, the Green Jacket kept on talking.

"If it was down to me, I'd be letting these guys shoot you. Buckler was one of theirs and you nearly killed him. Mallory says you can stay alive for now, so that's what happens. But if you try and escape, or do anything we don't like? Well, accidents happen."

Emma didn't reply, just played the part of the meek prisoner.

"You ask me, things are a bit soft round here," the Green Jacket carried on, and Emma could tell he was trying to convince himself. There was a note of something approaching fear in his voice. *Good.* "Someone attacks one of ours like that, they need to be made an example of. Stop the rest of your anarchist mates thinking they can get away with it. Lucky for you I don't give the orders."

The monologue continued as they descended in the lift and into the car park. Emma was led over to a black van and, while one of the guards was distracted by unlocking the van door, she took her chance. Jerking free of the remaining guard's grip, she dropped to her knees.

"What the hell?" the Green Jacket snapped. "What are you doing? Get up!"

"I can't!" Emma gasped, putting on the performance of her life. "Oh God, it's coming back! That thing…the thing that made me do it, it's coming back!"

"Get up," the Green Jacket repeated, grabbing hold of Emma's jacket.

It was then that Emma looked up, pulled the worst face she could manage and snarled, “Get your hands off me!”

For a second, the Green Jacket had no idea what to do. The two guards hung back by the van, looking at each other.

Emma pressed home her advantage. “I will snap these puny bonds and crush you.” *Puny? Nice one, Emma.* She was overcome by a sudden urge to giggle but stifled it and roared at the top of her voice, “NOW GET YOUR HANDS OFF ME!”

The startled Green Jacket let go. Emma leapt to her feet, barged him out of the way and made a run for the entrance of the car park. The fact that her hands were still tied behind her back made running awkward, but she forced her feet to keep moving.

“Stop her!” the Green Jacket yelled.

Behind her, Emma heard the guards fumble for their guns, but she gritted her teeth and carried on running, not looking back, thinking any second now she would hear a shot and that would be it. Instead, she heard the roar of an engine ahead of her and another car came up the entry ramp, cutting off her escape route. She came to a halt and stood there with her hands shackled behind her back and nowhere to run as the guards raised their weapons and took aim. The clack of safety catches being released echoed off the concrete walls. She shut her eyes and waited for the end.

Chapter Three

IN A DISUSED Tube tunnel underneath London, the atmosphere was electric with tension. Since work had resumed that morning, Richard Wells had waited and watched impotently as Carla Lockhart and her team carefully cut around the skeletal figure embedded in the wall. The team—a tall, blonde woman and two men—followed Lockhart's instructions to the letter. Wells didn't know their names. No-one had bothered to introduce him. A frame had been erected around the figure to keep it in place while the archaeologists worked. It had to be kept intact, Lockhart had said. It was no damn good to anyone in bits.

Not for the first time, Wells wondered what he had got himself into when he accepted this job. His training at Sandhurst and then his years of service in Britain and overseas had not really prepared him for this. Give him command of a unit under fire in Iraq and he was fine. Overseeing the teams trying to figure out what had happened in Trafalgar Square was within his comfort zone. Watching a bunch of archaeologists dig the corpse of an angel out of a wall was not something British Army training covered.

Not that Wells was completely convinced about the angel thing. It was like being sent on a mission to investigate the Loch Ness Monster. Angels, in Wells' experience, were a myth. He was used to dealing with people and facts. Yet this thing, whatever it was...its skeleton had something that looked very much like wings, and how did you explain that? There were things going on here that Wells didn't understand, things he wasn't being told, and he felt compelled to try and regain control of the situation before he was pushed to one side altogether.

"How's it going?" he asked, standing just behind Lockhart and trying to see over her shoulder.

"Slowly," she said. The look of concentration on her face reminded Wells of one his troops trying to defuse a roadside bomb. "We can't rush this, but I think we're nearly there. It has to come out in one piece or we might as well forget it."

"So..." Wells dropped his voice to a confidential level. "An angel? Really?"

"For want of another explanation, I'll stick with that for now. It looks like a man with wings, that much I know. Until we get it down and have a closer look, angel will do for me."

"But what about this idea of bringing that woman in to heal it? I can't see why you're getting involved in that."

"It's crazy." Lockhart stopped cutting for a moment. "Someone, somewhere is seriously unhinged. But if it keeps them happy..."

"I heard you witnessed her do it."

"I saw some damn thing, that's for sure. But I've seen magic shows too, and I know it isn't really magic. All I want to do is my job here. I could be involved in one of the most important historical finds since...well, since forever. If they want to play with faith healers, that's up to them. I just want to know what this is. So if you don't mind...?"

"Sorry. Yes, you carry on." Wells went back to watching. The tunnel was hot and airless, and he opened a bottle of water and took a long drink.

He'd been watching and waiting for another hour when suddenly one of Lockhart's team shouted, "That's it!" Wells hurried over, but Lockhart placed a hand on his chest to stop him.

"Keep back, please," she said. "This is where it could all go horribly wrong."

Wells stepped back and observed as the team carefully lifted the block of compacted clay containing the skeleton away from the wall.

"Steady! Steady!" Lockhart called. "Drop this and you're fired. Now easy..."

The team lowered the clay block onto a trolley that looked uncomfortably like a mortuary gurney, and then there were celebrations all round. Lockhart and the others hugged and high-fived each other.

"Is that it?" Wells asked. "Job done?"

"Job not even really begun yet," Lockhart told him, breaking away from the group. "Now the fun starts. We've got to get it out of the clay and find out what it is."

"Buxton and his higher-ups want to know when they can get a look at it."

"We're really not ready for the laying on of hands yet. It could be days before we get it out of the clay. Weeks even. You can't rush it. That thing is very fragile."

"I'll let him know. I don't think he'll be too happy."

"He can scream and shout and stamp his feet if he wants. He's brought me over here for my expertise so he'll have to listen to what I've got to say."

Anything further Lockhart might have had to say was interrupted by one of the men on her team.

"Carla, you need to see this!"

"What is it, Nathan?"

The man beckoned her over. She made a *there's always something* face to Wells and excused herself. Wells followed her over to the wall, which now had a large rectangular hole cut into it. Nathan was looking at something in the hole.

"Looks like there was something behind our feathered friend."

"Don't touch it," Lockhart ordered. "Let me see."

Wells followed Nathan's gaze and saw there was indeed the shape of a squareish object protruding from the inner wall of the hole.

"That looks like...a book?"

"Yes, it does," Lockhart agreed. "What in the hell is that doing there?"

Chapter Four

JOEY WOKE UP in a cell, and it took him a little while to remember how he'd got there. It came flooding back to him—the trip to his old house. The black Audi…

The car was already rolling by the time Joey noticed it. He pretended he hadn't seen it though and strolled casually around the corner. When the car followed him, he picked up his pace, glancing over his shoulder at the vehicle as it crawled behind him, hugging the kerb. Up ahead was the busier main road; if he could get to it, the traffic might delay the Audi and give him a chance to get away, but instead, he took the unexpected move of doubling back, making a pantomime of patting down his pockets as if he had forgotten something important. As he passed the car, the passenger door opened, as he knew it would, and a man in a green coat got out. Joey feigned shock.

"Mr. Cale?" the Green Jacket asked.

"Wh-what do you want?" Joey stammered.

"Joseph Cale?" the Green Jacket repeated. "I'd like you to come with me, please."

"But why? I haven't done anything wrong. I was just visiting someone…"

"Who were you visiting?"

"Just a friend. They weren't in."

"In that case, you'll be able to spare the time to come with me. *Now.*"

The Green Jacket opened the rear door of the car and gestured to Joey to get in. Joey protested once more, but the Green Jacket pushed on his back, forcing him to get in.

Perfect. With any luck, they were taking him to the same place they were holding Emma; he'd worry about how to get them both out of there later.

As they drove, the two Green Jackets—the one who had got out of the car and the driver—made no attempt to converse with Joey or each other. The Green Jacket in the passenger seat made a call to report they were on their way in, but he only spoke to 'Control', so it told Joey nothing about where they were headed. The tinted windows made it impossible to see, and Joey tried to keep track of the turns the car made but lost it after the first five and settled back in his seat, waiting until they reached their destination.

He wanted to take out his mobile to check the time but thought it was probably wisest not to. Raj would doubtless have noticed his absence by now and would almost certainly be trying to get hold of him. In any case, he didn't know when they had set off, so the time now would not really tell him anything.

After a while, the car stopped; Joey was dragged out of the back and hurried through a door before he had a chance to take in his surroundings. He was escorted down a corridor and shoved into this narrow, windowless cell. He was locked in, and, apart from being brought a cup of tea in a polystyrene cup and a stale biscuit by a silent Green Jacket, he had seen nobody since. The only vague concession towards furniture was a mattress on the floor and, after trying and failing to drink his tea, Joey lay down and surprised himself by going to sleep.

Now, it seemed to be morning, and all he could do was hope they weren't going to keep him here, wherever *here* was, but instead move him to wherever Emma was being held. He had no idea what he was going to do when he got there, but he could certainly do nothing stuck here.

Before he could wonder any further, the door was flung open, and two Green Jackets—possibly the same ones as last night—burst in. One stayed by the door while the other dragged Joey roughly to his feet. Then it was back down the corridor and outside, where another car was waiting. Once again, Joey was pushed into the back seat and the car sped off.

After what felt like maybe two, possibly three hours, the car suddenly slowed. This was clearly not a brief stop at traffic lights, because instead of smooth braking, the car was brought to a screeching halt that threw Joey forward so violently he hit his forehead on the back of the driver's seat.

The driver yelled, "Stay there!" at Joey, then he and his colleague slammed out of the car, almost, or so it seemed, taking the doors off as they went.

From inside the car, Joey couldn't see what was going on, only that they were in an underground car park, but there was a great deal of shouting followed by gunshots. In the confined space, they were deafening, which also made it hard to determine which direction they were coming from. Joey thought about ducking down in the foot well, but when a stray shot shattered the driver's side window and thudded into the dashboard, he decided he would probably be safer out of the car.

He waited until there was a brief pause in the shooting and cautiously opened the passenger side door, crouching low and hoping this would put the car between him and the armed assailant. Looking over his shoulder, he saw nothing but the open entrance. He'd judged correctly; whatever was going on was happening on the other side of the car. He half-stood to get a better view, but another bullet pinged off the roof, and he ducked his head again, spotting a sudden flurry of purple and black as something—*someone*—ran straight into him. He startled, and then startled again when he was suddenly somewhere else entirely with Emma Winrush in his arms.

She stepped back abruptly. "Joey! What—" She stopped and looked around. "Where the hell are we? What have you done?"

"Well, at least we don't have to worry about getting shot," Joey said casually, and then frowned as it dawned on him. *Emma's voice...* She didn't sound like the Emma he'd left in Formby woods. She sounded more like… He shook his head. It couldn't be. He tried to focus on their surroundings.

They were no longer standing next to a car. There were no Green Jackets shooting at them—no noise at all apart from the sound of their own breathing. They were in a dark tunnel carved out of rock, and Joey had a horrible, vertiginous feeling of déjà vu. There was the familiar reek of burning flesh, the same unearthly red glow coming from further down the tunnel. Somewhere nearby, cutting through the silence, was a low, barely audible whisper that raised goosebumps all over Joey's body. Emma must've heard it too; she was rubbing her arms in a way Joey hadn't seen in a while.

"They had me tied up back there," she explained.

"They're itching, aren't they?"

"Like crazy. He's here, isn't he?" she said. "Saunders."

Joey nodded. He wanted to ask how she knew but wasn't sure he was ready for the answer yet. Instead, he peered down the tunnel away from the red glow.

"This way," he said, taking her hand. "We really need to get out of here."

Chapter Five

RAJ WAS SITTING at Remick's bedside when his phone rang and woke him with a jolt. The dim light of early morning seeped in through the window, confirming he'd somehow slept through the night in the chair with Misha resting her head on his leg. He liked the loyalty she showed him. Whenever he was in his quarters, she stayed by his side and always behaved herself when he left, trusting he would come back. He didn't enjoy the damp feeling of her drool soaking into his trouser leg quite so much, but slobber came with the territory with a dog like Misha.

It was worth it, though; Raj would not be without her now. She had saved his life before, and would doubtless do so again if necessary. Ever since she'd been shot and he'd taken care of her—many months ago and on a different Earth altogether—she had been his and he hers.

When Raj's annoying but insistent ring tone sounded, she lifted her head and looked at him with doleful eyes. Clearly something within her associated the sound of his phone with him having to go out and leave her, and usually she was right.

"Sorry, babe," he said to Misha, disentangling himself from her and getting to his feet. His back was stiff from sitting in one position for so long, and he stretched as he crossed the room to his jacket, pulling out the phone and answering it just before it could go to voicemail.

"Raj?" said the voice of Billy Radley in his ear.

"Billy. What's up?"

"Can you come down to the garage? There's something you need to see."

"What is it? Can it wait, Bill?"

"I don't think it can. I can't explain on the phone. It's best if you come and see for yourself."

"Okay. Leave it with me."

Raj rang off and picked up his jacket. He went over to Misha, who was still waiting patiently by the bed, and stroked her head. She looked at him with liquid-brown eyes as if to say, *here we go again*.

"I know," Raj said. "I won't be long. Then maybe we could go for a walk." Misha's tail thumped the floor.

Remick stirred as Raj reached the door, and he waited for a second, in case Remick was just moving in his sleep, but then he groaned.

"Hang on," Raj said. "Don't try to move. You need to rest."

"No," Remick croaked. "Don't…go."

"I won't be long. Misha will look after you."

"Not…safe."

"I'll be fine. It's only Billy. Give me ten minutes and I'll be back."

Raj moved to go again, but Remick's hand shot out and grabbed his wrist. For someone in the state he was in, he gripped with a strength that surprised Raj. He looked down and saw that the skin on Remick's hand and arm, while still livid, looked better than it had before.

"What is it, Remick?" he asked. "What's wrong?"

"You need…to stay."

"Okay. Give me a minute."

Raj took his phone out again and called up one of his speed-dial numbers.

"Liza?" he said, when the call was answered. "Yes, good morning to you too. Do us a favour. I'm a bit tied up here, but Billy's getting into a lather about something down in the garage. … Yes, I know, but that's Billy, isn't it? Could you nip down and see what's up? … Give me a call if you need me. Thanks Liza."

Raj hung up and looked back at Remick.

"What's this about?"

"Saving...your life," Remick replied and smiled with cracked lips.

***

Billy Radley stood in the underground car park and waited. If the voice in his head was right, he would soon have the opportunity to put Chowdhury out of the picture once and for all. Since he had first heard the voice, Radley had been bristling with a confidence he had not felt for a long time. He had gone back to his quarters and sat up all night, waiting, feeling strength and power course through his veins—he could take on the world.

The world could wait, however. For the moment, it was just Chowdhury he was interested in. Radley felt the weight of the crowbar in his hand, heard the rustling of feathers amongst the rafters above his head and waited.

***

Liza Hunt had been half expecting Raj's call since Billy had phoned her last night and had spent much of the time since impatiently waiting in her quarters, trying to read a book, putting it down then picking it up again. If what Billy had said was true, and someone had used the hot code 'Remick', she wanted to be involved, not just hanging around while the boys had all the fun. In the end, she'd decided Raj had probably dealt with whatever it was and gone to bed.

It was typical he'd chosen to ring as soon as she was up and about to get into the shower. She'd turned on the hot water and nearly missed the call because of the noise. Luckily, she'd caught the screen flashing out of the corner of her eye before she had a chance to get undressed and under the shower.

As she headed down to the underground car park, she cursed Billy Radley. Whatever was bugging him was obviously not urgent enough for Raj to go himself, so instead Liza had to put off her shower and go and hold Radley's hand. She got on with Billy most of the time, but he had a needy side to him that irritated her. He felt entitled to the more interesting missions without actually doing that much to earn it. Liza, on the other hand, had worked hard and trained hard and fought for her place in the Catesby Foundation.

She'd been working in a pizza restaurant when the Catesbys found her, a walking cliché in a uniform. She was smart enough to do better for herself but had been denied the opportunities and education which were handed out to all the white, middle-class kids whose parents had a bit of money and nice houses and cars. Liza had been brought up by loving grandparents when her mother, who got banged up at eighteen by some bloke who hadn't hung around, had decided there was a better life elsewhere that didn't involve a child. Her grandparents had done their best, surrounding her with love, encouraging her to read books and work hard at school. But if Liza had wanted to go to university, there was no money to send her there, so it had never been a possibility. Instead, she had taken the first job she could get and drifted from one food or coffee chain to another, earning just enough to get by and give some back to her grandparents.

The day she was recruited by the Catesbys was pretty much like any other. The restaurant was busy with the lunchtime rush, and Liza was serving a table of four idiots from one of the local offices who were of the opinion they had the right to get drunk at lunchtime and harass the staff. She had taken about as much as she could of remarks about her figure, but when one of the men suggested if she didn't like it, she could go back to where she came from, Liza snapped. She tipped a plate holding a spicy meat feast into the customer's lap, threw her name badge onto the table and walked out.

It was only when she was standing outside it really sank in that she might now be out of work. As she stood wondering whether to go back in and apologise, a voice said, "That was an excellent shot." She turned, and saw, in a wheelchair in the restaurant doorway, a silver-haired woman, who was regarding Liza with a look of amusement.

"Look, if you've come to have a go at me too, then you should know I'm having a really bad day."

"No," replied the woman, whom Liza would soon come to know as Davina Watson. "I'm not here to give you a hard time. I want to offer you a job."

Three years later and Liza had given her life to the Catesby Foundation. Despite the progressive nature of the organisation, even they had far fewer female operatives than male, but she worked twice as hard as her male colleagues to prove her worth and believed that she had, time and time again. That was why people like Billy Radley annoyed her. Just like the other kids at school, he had that in-bred sense of entitlement to a respect Liza had earned through sheer hard work. As she descended in the lift to the car park, she was quite prepared to tell him that too.

She knew there was something wrong as soon as the lift door opened. It was too quiet. If there was really something going on, she'd have expected Radley to be waiting near the door, but there seemed to be no-one about. All she could hear was the sound of pigeons or something scratching about in the rafters, and she was beginning to wish she'd come armed.

Cautiously, she crept out of the lift, looking all round. "Billy? You there?"

There was no reply, so she went further into the car park, passing a row of vehicles. As she rounded a corner, she caught sight of a figure ahead of her. Although his back was turned, she recognised Billy Radley straight away.

"What's going on, Billy?" she asked, walking closer to him. It was then that she saw something really weird. He was standing next to the car Raj normally used, and there were three large seagulls perched on the roof. Billy seemed to be speaking to them.

"Not Chowdhury," he was saying. "Not him."

"Billy? You okay?" Liza called.

Radley turned to face her, and she gasped when she saw him. Half his face was a mask of blood which flowed freely from several wounds on his forehead. He hefted a crowbar in one hand and smashed it against the windscreen of the car, grinning as a spider's web of cracks spread out from the impact.

"Never mind," he said. "You'll do."

Chapter Six

WITH EMMA'S HAND in his, Joey felt something approaching hope for the first time since arriving on this world. Despite being in a pitch-black tunnel that was who knew where and the strong possibility Saunders was down there with them, Joey was not alone. There had been enough signs to allow him to believe this Emma was not the Emma Winrush belonging to this world, but somehow, miraculously, the Emma he had known; the one who had died. As they edged their way through the darkness, he could no longer keep silent about it.

"It *is* you, isn't it?"

"That depends," came the reply, and Joey recognised not just the voice but the intonations of it—subtle inflections which told him all he needed to know. "Who do you think I am?"

"You're Emma."

"Well, that's pretty obvious."

"*My* Emma."

"I'd go easy on the 'my' bit there, mate. But yes, I'm that Emma. The dead one."

"But how? How can you be? I saw you..." Joey broke off. He didn't want to say the word. Emma said it for him.

"Die? Yes, you did. Somehow, it's my mind in her body. But it's hers too. It's both of us. And is it just me, or is it weird calling someone who's me, 'her'?"

"I don't think I've ever heard anyone say anything weirder than that."

Through the darkness, Emma laughed. "So," she said, "where are the three of us going?"

"Out of here, hopefully."

They continued on along the tunnel for a while, Joey feeling the wall with one hand, the other hand keeping tight hold of Emma's.

"This had better lead somewhere," Emma said eventually. "It's so bloody dark."

"The old you would have had a lighter with her."

"Yes, well, this Emma doesn't smoke, and I don't really want her to start. I'll tell you what, though, if we come to a dead end, you're in trouble."

"It's better than going the other way. Unless you want to run into Saunders again."

"If he's here, why isn't he coming after us?"

"Something's happened to him. Last time I was down here, he didn't look in a fit state to walk. He was like…I don't know. Like a corpse someone had thrown on the fire."

"Good. I hope he's in a lot of pain."

They carried on in silence, but Emma's whole posture had stiffened, and Joey sensed the hatred for Saunders radiating from her.

"Of course," she said, "we could always go back and finish the job."

"What? Are you serious?"

"Well, if he's in such a bad state, why not? He's not going to fight back, is he? How do you kill a demon? Stake through the heart? Take his head off?"

"I don't know. I don't even know if you can kill something like him. I don't really want to get close enough to find out. He *killed* you, Emma."

"Yes, Joey. I know. The bastard has also been in my—Emma's—head. He's up to something. There's something he wants here."

"What?"

"I don't know. Somehow, I pushed him out of Emma's head before I could find out. But if he's after something that's going to make him stronger, don't you think we'd better stop him before he finds it?"

"Or find it first."

"Which is going to be dead easy when we don't know what it is. Nice one, Joey. You come up with some great ideas."

Joey laughed. "It's good to have you back, Emma."

She smiled at him, and it suddenly struck him that he could see it—more or less.

"It's getting lighter," he said.

"About time. Told you this was the right way."

Joey could now see the tunnel wall and took his hand away from it, wiping the damp off on his trouser leg. It was still very gloomy but light enough to see where they were going without having to feel their way. It also meant they could pick up their pace and walk faster.

"You could probably let go of my hand now, you know," Emma said. "I'm not going to fall over."

"You want me to?"

"No, you're okay." She gave his hand a squeeze. "Best to be safe."

They walked on like that for another ten minutes or so.

"I wonder what these tunnels are for?" Joey said. "They're man-made, I think."

"What makes you say that?"

"Look at the walls."

Emma glanced up and around. "It just looks like a tunnel to me."

"It's too regular. If this was natural, like underground caves or something, there would be all sorts of rocks sticking out. This has been dug out by people."

"Or the biggest mole you've ever seen."

"It reminds me of something. Maybe it's an old coal mine. Whatever it is, if people have dug it, there will be a way out. That light must be coming from somewhere. I think we're going the right way."

"Then what?"

"I don't know. There's a lot of stuff I need to tell you. I caught up with Raj and—"

"Yes, you told me when I was the other Emma. Is Raj that guy you were with at Pendle? Back in the other place? I didn't really get a chance to be introduced."

"No, of course you didn't. You'll like Raj. When we get out of here, I hope we can find him."

"So what's this stuff you need to tell me?"

As they walked, Joey told her about the Catesby Foundation and what he had learned there, and she filled in some of the blanks from the memories she had inherited from the other Emma, like how, in light of the Trafalgar Square disaster, the Green Jackets had suddenly appeared and seemed to be everywhere, holding the streets in a grip of fear, and how the rumours had started about people disappearing or being arrested and taken away for apparently no reason. Joey kept quiet while Emma repeated bits he had heard before.

"Does anyone know why the Green Jackets look like that?" he asked. "I mean, the jackets are one thing, but the hair and the shades…what's that all about? Does anyone know?"

"There are all sorts of theories on the net," Emma replied. "They're taken down almost as soon as they appear, but no, nobody seems to know for sure."

"Odd, that. It's a strange choice. Still, it makes them easier to spot." Joey stopped and pointed up ahead. "Hey, look! It's definitely getting lighter. It doesn't look like sunlight either. That's electric light, I'm sure of it."

He was about to set off again when Emma pulled him back.

"If that's electric light, then it means there could be people down here."

"Yes, it does. With a bit of luck, they might be able to tell us how to get out of here."

"You think? You said Saunders is down here. What if they're something to do with him?"

On one of the walls, a shadow appeared against the light—the elongated and unmistakable shadow of a person, which grew as it got nearer.

"I think we're about to find out," Joey said.

Chapter Seven

EVAN LOOKED FORWARD to Dr. Franklin's visits, but he didn't really want to tell her about the birds. He and Ruby liked Dr. Franklin. She was friendly and jolly and easy to talk to, and they always felt better after talking to her. She encouraged them to open up about what had happened to them after their mother had disappeared and seemed to understand about the horrible time when the burning man had got into Ruby's head and made her hurt Evan. Dr. Franklin said it wasn't Ruby's fault and didn't judge her for it. But there were some things Evan didn't want to tell her, at least, not until he was sure.

He and Ruby had been playing in Patrice's garden with Alex the first time he saw the birds. It had been a lovely day. The sun was shining and everybody was in a good mood. It was one of those days when all the trouble they had been through seemed a long way away. They could just play and not worry about whether the burning man might come back, or wonder why Joey didn't come to see them, or remember the last time they saw Emma, lifeless in Joey's arms. On a day like this, they just ran about and felt the warmth of the sun, and it was almost as if everything had happened to someone else.

It was only when Evan stopped running for a moment to catch his breath that he noticed the birds. Patrice had a big garden and there were always a lot of them around. Evan could even recognise some of them now because Patrice had told him what they were called, or sometimes Alex did if he knew.

Nobody had ever told Evan what birds were called before. He knew sparrows and pigeons, of course. *Everyone* knew them. He knew robins because they were on Christmas cards, and blackbirds were obvious because they were black. But is was Patrice who had told Evan these noisy, chattery birds were called starlings, and he'd thought they were black, too, at first, but when he'd looked closer or the sun caught their feathers, there were greens and purples and browns—not black at all.

Evan had never really liked the starlings, though. There were too many of them and they made such a racket. All the same, he didn't feel threatened by them—not until this day, when seven of them were lined up on the back wall of the garden. The fact they weren't making their usual chattering noises but instead just perched there silently was disturbing enough, but what really bothered Evan was the way they seemed to be watching him and Ruby. If they moved, the birds' heads all moved as one to follow them.

To prove a point, Evan did the thing where no-one could see him, the trick he had found he could do in that other place. He did the thing and moved to the other side of the garden. The birds carried on watching Ruby and took no notice of Evan at all. One even flew off. Evan went back to re-join his sister and their friend but kept glancing over at the birds. They stayed on the wall watching for a while; the next time Evan looked, they had gone.

He thought about the birds that night and had more or less convinced himself it was his imagination and that they couldn't really have been watching him. They were just stupid birds. He might not have worried about it at all if the starlings had not come back the next day. He couldn't be sure they were the same ones, of course. One starling looked very much like another, but when Evan took a bag of rubbish out to the bin the next morning, there were five of them standing side by side in silence on the roof of the garden shed.

It was almost as if they had been waiting for him to come out, and he considered doing the vanishing thing again, but this time they made him feel angry. He picked up a stone from the path and hurled it at the shed. It didn't get anywhere near them but rattled off the roof and bounced into one of the flower beds. Startled by the noise, the birds flew off with a shrill squawk. Evan watched them go and then went back inside. At least he knew he could scare them away any time he wanted to, but at the back of his mind was a thought he couldn't shake—a thought that scared him for reasons he couldn't put into words. The birds knew where he was.

A few days later, Dr. Franklin came for one of her regular visits. As usual, Patrice made a cup of coffee for Dr. Franklin and a glass of squash each for Evan and Ruby. Dr. Franklin took the children into the front room—the room Patrice only used for important visitors—and closed the door. She sat in an armchair and, as usual, Evan and Ruby sat side by side on the settee.

"Now then," Dr. Franklin began. "How have you both been?"

"Fine, thank you, Dr. Franklin," Evan replied politely.

"That's good. What about you, Ruby?"

"Fine, thank you," Ruby said, nearly inaudibly.

"Nothing you want to tell me about?"

The children looked at each other and shook their heads in unison. Evan tried to look back at Dr. Franklin but found he couldn't and looked at the floor instead.

"Are you all right, Evan? Has something happened?"

"No. Nothing."

"Okay. I've got to ask, you know that, don't you? Just to make sure everything's okay."

Evan didn't reply.

"Well, anyway, I've got some good news for you. We've found your friend Joey Cale, and he said he would love to see you. Would you like to see him?"

Evan looked up, hardly able to believe his ears.

"Really?" He saw Ruby was grinning too. "We can go and see him? When?"

"How about now? I've asked Patrice, and she said it's absolutely fine if I take you to see Joey right now. What do you think?"

Before Evan could reply, Ruby exclaimed, "Yes please!" and jumped to her feet.

"Well, okay!" Dr. Franklin laughed. "Why don't you get your coats and we'll go?"

Dr. Franklin opened the door, and Evan and Ruby ran out into the hall, where Patrice was waiting.

"We're going to see Joey!" Evan said. Then he stopped. "Is that okay, Patrice?"

"It's fine," Patrice replied. "Dr. Franklin will look after you, but you must do exactly what she says."

"We will!"

Patrice gave Dr. Franklin an anxious look. "Are you sure about this? They haven't been out much since they got here."

"Patrice, don't worry so much. We're not going far, and they've been dying to see Joey again. We'll be back in an hour or so. Two hours tops." Dr. Franklin stooped slightly to address Evan and Ruby, who had now put on their coats. "Give Patrice a hug, guys, and then we'll get off."

Ruby threw her arms around Patrice, and when she had finished, Evan followed suit. Then Dr. Franklin led them out of the front door.

"Where are you parked?" Patrice asked as she waited on the front doorstep.

"Just around the corner. We'll be back very soon. You put your feet up and enjoy the peace and quiet for once."

As Dr. Franklin led the children down the road to the corner, Evan turned once and waved to Patrice. Afterwards, he would remember the sight of her standing on the step, waving to them and looking strangely sad.

As they rounded the corner, Dr. Franklin pointed to a big black car that was parked on the other side of the road.

"There we go," she said. "A friend of mine is waiting in the car to take us to Joey."

Evan suddenly felt nervous. It was enough of a surprise they were going to see Joey at all, but he'd thought it would just be them and Dr. Franklin. He hadn't expected there to be anyone else. By the time Dr. Franklin had opened the car door and ushered Evan and Ruby inside, it was too late to go back, even when they caught sight of the man in the green coat sitting in the driver's seat.

"This is my friend Mr. Webb," Dr. Franklin said. "I'm afraid Joey is going to have to wait. There's something much more important for you to do first."

Chapter Eight

MARTIN BUXTON SAT at his desk, staring into space and chewing one of the indigestion tablets he needed more and more these days. He'd just put the phone down after a lengthy conversation and needed to consider its implications. He hadn't enjoyed the call one bit.

There was a time when he would have relished the status he had been awarded. When he had first put on his constable's uniform and helmet, nearly thirty years ago, he little suspected that one day he would be the occupant of such a luxurious office and on good terms with the Home Secretary. Yet here he was, and the responsibilities and demands that came with the office were sometimes a heavy burden to carry. He had just given the order to have two young children uprooted from a house in which they felt safe, by someone they trusted. That was bad enough, but the reasons why it had happened and the purpose for which the children were to be used hardly bore thinking about. It was on days like this Buxton had to keep reminding himself why he was doing this job at all.

When he first joined the police, he was surprised to find his fellow recruits had widely different reasons for their career choice. Some were doing it for want of anything else to do. There were some who had chosen the police as an outlet for their aggression—a way they could throw their weight around and get paid to do so. Buxton found he was part of a minority of new constables who had joined the force in the hope of making a difference.

He had neighbours who had experienced the trauma of coming home to find someone had broken into their house. A lad he knew vaguely at school had gone out for the night and been beaten so badly they had spent what remained of their life in a vegetative state hooked up to an array of machines.

The young Constable Buxton had wanted to do what he could to prevent anyone else from going through nightmares like those. He'd wanted to uphold the law and had spent his career in the same mind, progressing up the ranks, competing against other officers who had come in at degree level and achieved rank without experience. Over the years, he had endured riots and an increasing mistrust of the police but had maintained a belief that what he was doing was right and necessary.

It was this belief that meant he'd said yes immediately when asked to take charge of the investigation into probably the worst and certainly the highest profile human disaster his country had faced. Britain had been through two world wars with a much higher body count, and there had been other tragedies that had cost more lives, but the attack on Trafalgar Square had been one of the most significant events in generations because of what it represented and the outrage it caused. A still unknown number of British people had been killed on British soil, and answers were being demanded by the country and indeed the world.

But Buxton rapidly discovered he had been handed what was usually referred to as a poisoned chalice. What he was being expected to lead wasn't so much a criminal investigation as a public relations exercise, or, at least, that was what the powers-that-be called it. As far as Buxton was concerned, it was quite possibly the biggest cover-up the country had ever seen.

The Government, who had been under considerable pressure to take a harder line on crime, had taken the opportunity which the disaster handed to them, and used it to set up the Special Powers Executive—the SPX as the officials called it, or the Green Jackets to everyone else. The green uniforms were created by a public relations firm to look distinctive and quasi-military. It had, apparently, started as a joke in response to accusations in the left-wing press that Britain was setting up its own version of the SS, but someone somewhere rolled with it.

The look was surprisingly effective, although Buxton personally thought the sunglasses were a step too far, and made the Green Jackets look like wannabe rock stars, but it wasn't his decision to make. His job was to find out what had really happened at Trafalgar Square and contain that information to make sure it never got out.

The truth was, he still didn't know the answer. Yes, something had come out of the sky and exploded, and there should have been evidence as to what that something was. A missile would have left debris, shrapnel, but it was as if whatever had hit the Square had vaporised on impact, and the experts Buxton had spoken to all agreed on one thing: no country in the world had that kind of technology.

So either one of Britain's enemies had technology that had been kept secret up until now or there was another explanation nobody had been able to provide. With none of the usual suspects taking credit for the attack, the latter seemed more likely, and it gave Buxton a huge problem. It raised the possibility that whatever it was had not come from this world at all, and that possibility was wrapped up in a whole other set of protocols. The Home Office wanted answers, and so far, Buxton had none to give.

When the Home Secretary had phoned this morning, Buxton had expected another dressing-down about how slowly the investigation was progressing. Instead, the call was about two children who were being brought to the SPX's facility under Canary Wharf. They were essential, Buxton was told, to the SPX's ongoing operation to dismantle the Catesby Foundation, against whom successive Governments had been waging unsuccessful war for generations. It wasn't something Buxton wanted to be involved in. Any operation that involved planting an SPX operative to pose as a psychologist to extract information from children was contrary to all the reasons he had joined the police in the first place.

The Home Secretary was also getting into a flap—a fitting pun—over the 'birdman' that had been found. Because of its location, that *did* fall under Buxton's jurisdiction, much as he might wish it didn't. He thought it was an unnecessary distraction, probably a hoax someone had set up years ago and forgotten about, but the Home Office viewed it as something else that needed explaining, and fast.

The pressure was mounting on Buxton, and on Richard Wells too, to provide answers. What Buxton didn't appreciate was that while he wanted to find the perpetrators and take them swiftly through the judicial system, the Home Office, the Home Secretary in particular, wanted the *right* answers—answers which fitted with conclusions that had already been determined but nobody was prepared to reveal. That wasn't how policing worked, but Buxton's very generous salary made it unwise to raise too many arguments.

As he pondered which direction to take next, he was disturbed by the incongruously jaunty ringtone of his phone. He glanced at the number on the screen and his heart sank. He was tempted not to answer, but the caller would keep trying, so he accepted the call.

"Commander Mallory. What can I do for you?"

"You need to get down here right now," Mallory replied, her voice harder than normal, if that were possible.

"I'm a bit tied up. Can it wait?"

"No, Mr. Buxton. It can't wait. We have a situation here that could cost us all our jobs."

"Well, might I remind you, Commander, seeing as I technically outrank you, perhaps a request might have been more appropriate than a summons. If you have a *situation*, as you call it, surely that is for you to sort out. I really don't see what it has to do with me—"

"It has everything to do with you, or more accurately, it has everything to do with whatever the hell your people have found under the Square. I suggest you make yourself available and get here before I go over your head." With that, Mallory ended the call.

Buxton sighed. The acid indigestion was back and burning a hole in his chest. Some days, this nice office and the salary that went with it were really not worth it. He would have given anything to be back in uniform pounding the beat.

Chapter Nine

AS SOON AS Liza Hunt saw the look on Billy Radley's face and the blood oozing out from the wound on his forehead, she knew he wasn't just having a bad day at the office. She wondered at first if it was some kind of stress-related breakdown, but when he advanced on her, casually swinging a crowbar backwards and forwards, she no longer cared what was causing him to behave like that. She just knew she had to get out of there and warn Raj as quickly as possible.

She backed away towards the lift but kept her eye on the entrance to the car park. It was only a rectangle of light from her position, and she would have to go past Radley to get to it, but she could not allow him to gain access to the lift, and from there to the facility. She stopped backing away, and decided to try reason instead. Although she agreed in principle with the Foundation's policy of not arming its operatives, she couldn't help but think a gun would be useful right now.

"Billy, it's me. It's Liza. I don't know what the matter is, but whatever it is..."

"I know who you are," Radley answered, sounding dangerously calm. "I was hoping Chowdhury would come down here, but you'll do for now. I'll get him later."

"What's going on, Billy? Something's obviously upset you. Let's talk about it."

"Upset? *Upset*?" Each time he repeated the word, he punctuated it by smashing the crowbar into the front grille of Raj's car. "I'm not upset. I'm just taking what I deserve."

"You really need to get that cut on your head seen to. It looks nasty." Liza risked taking a step towards him, but he stopped her by raising the crowbar and pointing it at her chest. One good swing and she'd be seriously hurt at the very least.

"You don't want to do this, Billy. Whatever's going on, we can deal with it."

"Of course I want to do this! I've been wanting to do this for a long time."

There was a sudden, violent flapping, and the biggest seagull Liza had ever seen descended from the rafters and landed on the roof of Raj's car, joining the others that had been perched there since Liza arrived. They were not at all perturbed by the presence of humans, nor by the noise of Radley's assaults on the car. Liza found their stillness very unsettling. Whatever Radley planned to do next, he had a really creepy audience.

Radley moved a pace closer. The tip of his crowbar was now touching the front of Liza's sweatshirt, and she felt its point through the fabric. She took a breath, then grabbed the bar, pulling with all her might. It caught Radley by surprise but, determined not to surrender his weapon, he clung on. The forward momentum shifted him off balance, and Liza was finally able to do something she had been tempted to do quite frequently: she planted the toe of her boot squarely and firmly in his groin.

Radley cursed and went down like a sack of potatoes, dropping the crowbar. Liza kicked it away as hard as she could, then took off at a sprint towards the garage entrance, glancing over her shoulder as she ran. Radley was still struggling to get up. He was a long way behind her, but the same couldn't be said for two of the gulls, which had taken off from the roof of Raj's car and were rapidly gaining on her, the beating of their wings echoing unnaturally off the concrete walls of the car park.

Liza whipped off her jacket as she ran and swung it at the closest gull. The bird squawked and tried to wheel away from the attack but only succeeded in colliding almost comically with the other gull. There was a flurry of feathers as the two birds turned on each other with beaks and talons, and Liza made it out of the garage into the open air.

Outside, she made a quick decision and ran full pelt across the road, narrowly avoiding being hit by a van. The driver hammered on his horn and yelled some choice insults out of his window. Liza ignored him and ran into the scrap-metal yard, unwittingly following the path Billy Radley had taken the previous evening. Once she was sure she was out of sight, she ducked down behind one of the stacks of decaying cars and fumbled in her jacket for her phone, praying to anything listening that she hadn't dropped it when she hit the gull. A wave of relief washed over her as she located it, still in the inside pocket where she usually carried it.

She peered through a gap between two of the cars. From her vantage point, she could see across the road to the car park's entrance. Billy Radley came limping out and stopped, looking left and right. Liza ducked down behind the cars again and dialled Raj's number, muttering, "Come on, come on!" as it rang. Finally, Raj answered.

"Liza. Are you okay? What's going on?"

"Don't talk, just listen. You need to send a couple of people down to the car park. Billy Radley's gone nuts."

"Billy? What the... Wait there. I'm coming down."

"No! You stay where you are, do you understand? It's you he's after. Send Devon Rees and maybe Lily Park. They'll be able to handle him. I'll back them up but don't you come. Promise?"

"I should be there, Liza."

"You've got to promise. Send Dev and Lily."

"Okay. Whatever you say. But there had better be a good reason for this."

"If there is, I'm damned if I know what it is. Oh, and tell them to watch out for the bloody birds."

Liza hung up and went back to her vigil. Radley was still standing outside the entrance, looking this way and that but not moving. Once, she was almost certain he looked straight at her, but then he looked away again. All the while, he seemed to be talking to himself, keeping up some kind of agitated monologue, waving the crowbar, which he had apparently found again.

He's really lost it. Liza was momentarily surprised by a feeling of pity but shook it off by remembering the look of sheer hatred she had seen on his face. Before she could think any more, there was a metallic clang behind her. She whirled around to find several more gulls had landed on the scrap metal and were regarding her with naked hostility. Without taking her eye off them, she groped around and grabbed hold of a twisted piece of metal that had fallen off one of the cars.

"Right, you little bastards. This time I'm ready for you."

She approached the gulls, waving the metal in front of her like a sword.

"Well, come on! Come on!"

The gulls stared at her and made angry noises, but as she got up close to them, they took off and swooped away, low across the water. Liza threw the piece of metal onto the ground and brushed her hands together to get rid of the rust-coloured muck coating them. As she started back to her hiding place, she realised her shouts had attracted the attention of a couple of the workers from the scrapyard, who were watching with amusement.

"Jesus, girl," one said, "what did they do to you?"

"Crapped on my car," Liza replied and looked over the road to the car park entrance. Billy Radley was still outside, but a shout from inside made him turn and head back in. Now feeling bolder after her confrontation with the gulls, Liza strode back through the yard and across the road to finish the job.

She walked up to the entrance, quietly and cautiously, and peered inside. Radley had his back to her and was waving his crowbar at Dev Rees and Lily Park, who were trying to reason with him.

"You don't have to do this, man," Dev was saying. "Come 'head, Bill, you're one of us."

"Walk away, Rees," Radley answered. "This doesn't concern you. I want Chowdhury and that Hunt bitch."

"You've got her," Liza said, creeping up behind him and seizing him in a head-lock. He struggled, but Liza hooked a leg around his and slammed him face first to the floor. The crowbar flew from his hand and clanged onto the concrete.

"Your little mates aren't going to help you now," she said, planting a knee in the small of his back to keep him down, as Dev and Lily hurried over to help. "But then, you never did have much luck with the birds, did you?"

Chapter Ten

RAJ FINISHED HIS phone conversation with Liza, then strode over to the bed, where Remick was now sitting up, sipping a glass of water. The burns on his face were fading at an astonishing rate, and he now looked more like someone who had spent too long in the sun.

"I'd ask for something stronger, but I doubt you'd let me have it," he said.

Raj ignored the comment and snapped, "What the hell's going on, Remick? One of our people has just tried to attack another, who happens to be a good friend of mine. Apparently, it was me he was after."

"I told you I was saving your life."

"That's cold. I don't work like that. I don't put someone else in danger to save my own skin."

"You might have to." Remick took another long swig of the water, coughed and put the glass down. "You're important, Raj. You and the others who don't belong on this world. Anything else is—what's the term?—collateral damage."

"That's unacceptable. I won't have good people getting hurt for my sake."

"You might not have any choice there, I'm afraid. This is bigger than them, bigger than any of us. Your loyalty to the Catesbys does you credit. I'm glad they found you. We started the Foundation, by the way, a long time ago. We thought they might be handy."

"You did? My God, you're doing it again, aren't you? You're moving us like pawns on a chessboard. You did it at Pendle, and you're doing it again now. And you lied to us, Remick. Back at

Crosby beach. You said these other worlds were just experiments, backups, but they're not, are they?"

"No, they are exactly what I said. I just underplayed how many and how fully formed most of them are. They're not perfect by any means. On this one, for example, I wouldn't try to get to Market Harborough because it isn't there. Or Greenland."

"I want the truth, Remick. I want to know what's going on. Liza was attacked by seagulls, for God's sake. What's that all about?"

"Seagulls. That's reassuring."

"What's reassuring about that? They're all over the bloody place!"

"Yes, but if he's resorting to cheap party tricks, he's not strong enough to do anything much himself."

"Saunders, you mean."

"Yes, Raj. Saunders. Possessing lesser species is easy. Possessing people is pretty easy too, actually. It means Saunders' mind is active but his body isn't. I'm not surprised. I did some damage to him when we fought—"

"But he still beat you."

"Yes, he did. He's stronger than me usually. Time was, I could have beaten him in an instant. I did. That's how he came to be imprisoned where you found him. But I'm not what I was. I chose to relinquish a lot of my power a while ago. That's why I need help."

Raj thought for a moment. "So what?" he asked. "What now?"

"We need to stop him."

"Stop him doing what? What does he want?"

"Oh the usual, I would imagine. Revenge. Power. That sort of thing."

"Great. And we're caught in the middle. Thanks, Remick."

"You also have another problem. I sense another one of our kind is on this world. A lesser one, I think, but probably working for Saunders. They may have been hiding in plain sight here for a while."

"Do you know who?"

"I wish I did. I can probably find them, given time, but my power is not what it was. Find Saunders and you'll probably find all the answers you need. What I don't know is what he is doing here of all places. Of all the worlds and times, why here? There must be something he wants. It's not his freedom because he has that."

"Well, if you don't know—"

"I'll have to find out." Remick leaned back against the pillow and closed his eyes.

"Remick? Are you okay?"

Remick put a finger to his lips.

Realising he was getting nowhere, Raj got up and went to get some food for Misha, who had been sitting patiently waiting.

"One of these days, girl..." Raj spooned the food into her bowl. "One of these days, we'll settle down and have a nice, quiet life."

Misha wagged her tail in reply and wolfed the food down. Raj watched her fondly until his phone rang again—Davina Watson. That was a call he wasn't sure he wanted to take, but he answered it anyway.

"Raj, I want some answers," she demanded without preamble. She sounded more pissed off than Raj had ever heard her. "I want to know why Billy Radley is on his way to a cell. I want to know who that man is you have in your quarters. And I want to know where Joey Cale is."

"Joey? He's—"

"He's not here, Raj. While you've been doing whatever the hell it is you've been doing since last night, Joey Cale went walkabout. Get your arse down here *right now* and sort this out."

"I'll be right there," Raj said, but he was interrupted by a cry from the bed. He hung up on Davina and rushed over. Remick was sitting rigidly upright, a look of anguish on his face.

"Remick? What's the matter?"

Remick opened his eyes, and Raj saw something he had never seen in them before: fear.

"That was a bad idea," Remick said.

"What was a bad idea?"

“I had to find him. I had to see what he’s doing.” Remick reached out and took hold of Raj’s wrist. “But now he knows where I am, Raj. You have to get out of here. Take Misha and go.”

“But—”

“*Now*!”

The urgency in Remick’s voice silenced any argument. Raj grabbed his jacket and called Misha to him.

“Will you be okay?” he asked.

“Doesn’t matter. Go!”

With Misha at his heels, Raj raced from the room. From somewhere nearby, he heard glass breaking and screams, and as he turned a corner, he saw the source of the noise. Several windows had been smashed, and Raj was faced with the surreal site of a corridor filled with shrieking seagulls attacking anyone who got in their way. Misha began to growl and move towards the fray, but Raj grabbed her and held her back. Then he heard a voice behind him.

“Raj, get out of here!”

Remick, still unsteady on his feet, had followed him and was leaning with one hand on the wall.

“Don’t let him get the book!”

“Book? What—” Raj stopped uncertainly. “Come with me! I’ll jump us out of here.”

“No. It’s me they want,” he said, then shouted, “I’m over here!”

“Remick, don’t be stupid!”

“Get out, Raj. Go!”

The air above Raj’s head filled with birds as the gulls abandoned everything and everyone else and converged on Remick. Raj watched powerlessly as his friend was covered in screaming gulls, their white feathers becoming flecked with red as they pecked and pecked. At first, Remick fought back, sending several of the birds crashing in flames into the wall. The stench of burning feathers took over the corridor. But as more and more gulls flooded in through the broken window and joined the attack, Remick was soon overwhelmed.

Beneath the squawks of the birds and the flapping of wings, Raj heard Remick crying out what sounded like 'Angie', then it trailed off and stopped altogether. Choking back a wave of nausea, Raj took hold of Misha, pictured himself elsewhere and jumped, leaving his friend to die.

Chapter Eleven

"Hello? Is somebody there?" The voice echoed down the tunnel.

Joey and Emma flattened themselves against the wall and held their breath. The beam of a flashlight played around the tunnel walls and floor but missed them, this time at least.

"This is a restricted area!" the voice called again. "You shouldn't be down here. Come on. I'll show you the way out."

"There's no-one there, Nath," a second, female voice said. "I think you imagined it."

"I didn't," the first voice protested. "I saw someone, Marianne. I heard them moving about."

"Probably a rat. There must be hundreds of them down here."

"If it's a rat, it's a bloody big one."

"Come on. We'd best be getting back. You don't want to miss Sleeping Beauty waking up."

"Yeah, like that's going to happen."

The voices receded as the speakers moved away, back up the tunnel. Joey and Emma waited until they could no longer hear them, then both breathed out simultaneously.

"They've gone," Joey whispered.

"Yes, but what do we do now?" Emma wondered. "We can't go back if you reckon Saunders is lurking around, and we can't go this way because of them…"

"I think they were leaving. If we just hang on here for a bit…" Joey leaned back against the wall and took his phone out of his pocket.

"Who are you calling?" Emma asked, shielding her eyes with her hand. The screen was bright down here.

"No-one apparently," Joey put his phone away. "No signal."

"Pity you didn't think about your phone before. You know, when we were in the *pitch-black*?"

"I forgot. I thought about trying Raj, seeing as I just walked out on him. I thought he might be able to help."

"Looks like you're stuck with me." Emma didn't meet his eyes. Joey had never seen her even approaching shy before.

"I think I can cope with that," he said, putting his hand on her shoulder. She looked up at him and smiled. "Let's see about getting out of here."

With Joey in the lead, they headed off up the tunnel in the direction of the light, moving as quietly as they could, keenly aware of the sound of every loose stone they kicked as they went. The first time it happened, it was Emma whose foot dislodged a stone, which bounced off the wall with a sound like a quiet gunshot. Joey turned back and shushed her, and she whispered an apology. The next time, it was Joey who did, and it was Emma's turn to say, "Shhh!"

When the next stone pinged off the wall, it could have been either of them. It had now become inexplicably hilarious, and they had to stop for a moment while they got over a fit of the giggles. In the end, Joey said, "Well, if they hadn't heard us before, they probably have now," and suddenly it was serious again. The light up ahead was getting brighter and was emanating from somewhere around the next bend. They kept close to the tunnel wall and stopped; Joey gestured to Emma to stay where she was and went on ahead around the corner.

He entered a much wider section of tunnel, but it was obvious this was where the people had come from. There was scaffolding erected against one wall, with bright halogen lamps attached to the bars. Next to the scaffold was a workbench with an array of tools and empty takeaway coffee cups. Joey went over to the bench and picked up a trowel, inspecting it as if it might give him some clue as to its purpose.

Something, and he wasn't sure what, drew him to a nearby wall, which had a rectangular hole cut out of it that was slightly taller than he was and half as wide again. He reached out and touched the surface inside the hole. It felt damp and slightly slimy, solidified clay probably, but there was something else, a feeling Joey couldn't identify. It was like a vibration but not quite, a hum that went through his fingertips and made his heart beat faster. There was something like a whispering in the back of his head, and he snatched his hand away.

"What the hell do you think you're doing here?"

At the question, Joey spun round to find a tall, blonde woman dressed in overalls and carrying a flashlight—currently not switched on—in one hand and an iPad in the other.

"Nathan was right, wasn't he?" she said. "That was you he heard. What exactly are you doing down here?"

"Sorry," Joey replied, thinking fast. "It's just…well…me and my girlfriend were looking for somewhere private, you know? We sort of got lost."

"Your girlfriend's down here too?"

"Yes, she is. Emma?" When he called, Emma appeared from around the corner and did an embarrassed half-wave. "I was just saying how we got lost when we came down here—"

"For a snog, right?" the woman interrupted. "How did you get down here?"

"I don't know," Emma answered. "Like Joey said, we got lost."

The woman snorted a laugh. "Nice try. Before I call security, maybe you'd like to tell me the truth. For a start, she doesn't really look your type. More importantly, nobody, but nobody gets down here. You don't just get into the most heavily guarded bloody place in London for a snog and a selfie."

Joey glanced at Emma, who had now joined him. She shrugged. "She's right," she said. "You're not really my type."

The woman consulted her iPad and then looked back at Joey and Emma. "Do you know what? You're damn lucky it was me who came back and not Nathan. He'd have had security down on you straight away."

"How do you mean, lucky?" Joey asked.

"Because I'd guess we're not the only ones looking for you, Joey Cale. How come you went missing in Liverpool only a couple of hours ago and show up here? And for future reference, if you're going to get caught sneaking about a secure government site, you're better off not using your own names."

"So hang on," Emma said. "Does that mean you're—"

"Catesby, yes. Marianne Bond. Now we've got to find a way of getting you out of here. I can't afford to be caught with you. I've worked too hard to keep my cover, and I'm not having you blow it. I've got to get you somewhere safe before anyone else from the team gets down here."

She looked around, weighing up the options.

"How *did* you get here, anyway? To get here that fast, you must have flown!"

"Yes, sort of," Joey answered.

"No, actually, don't tell me. I really don't want to know. Okay, here's what we do. You need to hide. I'll see if I can smuggle some spare coveralls, try and make it look like you're with the team, at least 'til we get to the top. Anyone else comes down here in the meantime, you're on your own, understand?"

"Yes," Joey said. "Thanks."

"Don't thank me yet. There's a lot that could go wrong with this, and if it does, I'll deny all knowledge. Wait here."

"What's going on down here?" Joey asked. "Are you looking for something?"

"You really don't know? I thought that's why you're here. It's just the usual—you know, dead angels buried in the wall, that sort of thing. Now hide, for God's sake. I'll be as quick as I can."

She hurried away up the tunnel, leaving Joey and Emma stunned where they were.

"Did she just say 'dead angels'?" Emma asked.

"Yes, she did. And what do you mean, I'm not your type?"

Chapter Twelve

COMMANDER ANNA MALLORY looked through the inspection hatch in the door at the woman who was hunched up in the corner, trying to make herself as small as possible. From the look of the pathetic, cringing specimen in the cell, it was hard to understand what the fuss was all about, yet there seemed to be a shitstorm going on, and Mallory was caught right in the middle of it. That was not a place she wanted to be, and she fully intended to find out who was responsible for placing her there and kick their arse for them. She slammed the inspection hatch shut and turned to Martin Buxton, who was waiting for her in the corridor and looking distinctly murderous.

"I'm glad you found the time to see me, Mr. Buxton," she said. "It's a bit late, as it happens, but never mind."

"This is an ongoing situation, Commander," Buxton replied. "I have orders which override any local problems you have here."

"So let me see if I've got this straight." Mallory kept her voice level and calm. "The Government, who, at the end of the day, sign your pay cheque and mine, has instructed you to take time out from investigating the most highly publicised atrocity ever to be committed on these shores, just so I can turn the woman in that cell over to your custody. Is that right?"

"That is correct, yes."

"That woman, who, when she was brought here, I was given to believe is a huge threat to national security?"

"Yes."

"Well, I'm sorry, Mr. Buxton, but I have a few problems with that." Mallory began to count off on her fingers. "*One*, if she is the threat to national security she's supposed to be, I can't have her running around in your custody or anyone else's. She needs to be here. *Two*, when you took her out of here the other day, I heard she got involved in some cheap bloody conjuring trick, making out she can heal people by touching them. Now, you and I both know that's ridiculous, so we can't have that sort of thing going on. If it gets out we'll be a laughing stock."

"It was no trick. She—"

"And *three*, we've all got much bigger things than that to worry about, like how some teenage kid knew about your lot finding something under Trafalgar Square, why she put on a pantomime voice and ordered me to leave it alone, and where the hell she is now. I presume you know the Winrush girl is no longer in our custody? She apparently disappeared into thin air. So, we have one person out there somewhere with known connections to the Catesby Foundation and in possession of some very classified information and now I'm supposed to hand over another known associate of the Catesbys so you can lose her too. How am I doing so far?"

There was a lengthy silence while Buxton digested that tirade. Then he sighed deeply.

"Have you finished, Commander? Because I suggest you shut up for a minute and listen." He counted on his fingers too. "*One*, I think you need to remember the chain of command here. The order to turn that woman over to me came from much higher up than either of us could see if we stood on a chair, so I'm not going to argue with it and neither are you.

"*Two* it was no trick. Don't ask me to explain it because I can't, but she did heal that man. I witnessed it, so unless you're calling me an idiot or a liar, you'll just have to take my word for it.

"And *three*—and this is something I really suggest you remember—the Winrush girl was supposedly in the custody of your own SPX officers when she escaped, so I really wouldn't be shouting too loudly about that if I were you. Unless you get the prisoner ready for me in, say, half an hour, a report will be going in, indicating you possess an attitude that makes you unfit to hold rank and you'll be working out the rest of your career behind a desk. Is that clear?"

Mallory didn't reply but her expression was pure malice.

"Is that clear, Commander?" Buxton repeated.

"Yes," she said reluctantly. "Yes, it is."

"Good. Half an hour. And Commander, next time you think about phoning to summon me here and sort out your problems for you, I would suggest thinking again."

Buxton turned on his heel and walked away without waiting for any further reply. Mallory watched him all the way down the corridor before turning her attention to the cell door. She unholstered her sidearm, operated the door lock and stepped inside.

The air in the cell was rank with sweat and other odours Mallory really didn't want to contemplate. The woman in the corner didn't stir when the door opened, just stayed huddled, staring at the floor, or at nothing.

"I hope you realise the trouble you're causing me," Mallory said. Still nothing. "On your feet. I need you out of here."

The woman slowly looked up this time, strands of her dark hair glued to her face with sweat. There were dark bags under her eyes and her skin was deathly pale. She looked for all the world like every substance abuser Mallory had ever seen slowly killing themselves on the streets.

"You're me," she said, fixing Mallory with unfocused eyes.

"Hardly. Now, up you get. And while you're at it, why don't you do a bit of healing on yourself? Shouldn't be a problem for one of your talents."

"Doesn't work like that," the other Anna said softly.

"Doesn't bloody work at all if you ask me."

"What made you so hard?"

Mallory was taken aback by the question and replied before she could think.

"You want to try being me," she said.

"I have. It didn't work out like that."

Mallory crossed the cell and took hold of the other woman's face. She wasn't gentle about it. She didn't feel gentle. "You're nothing like me. You might look a bit like me, but you're not me."

"I am." The face might have been paler, with lines in different places to the ones Mallory counted in the mirror every day, but the eyes… It was the eyes.

"I'll tell you what happened to me. I got a job. I got a job I cared about and wanted to do the best I could. If I'm hard, it's because I have to be. This country is full of scumbags who want to hurt ordinary, decent people. I do what I do to protect those decent people. If the scum get themselves killed in the process, it's just a few less of them on the streets, isn't it? No loss. What would you do?"

"I did do it," said the other Anna Mallory. "I worked day and night in A and E trying to fix them all. The decent people *and* the scumbags."

"More fool you, then. Speaking of which, your talent for fixing people is needed somewhere else, so get on your feet and wash your face. It's time you were moving."

Mallory watched the other Anna shuffle over to the small sink in the corner of the cell, throw some water on her face and blindly fumbled for a paper towel and thought *I do that every morning.* The only difference being that Mallory did it in a nice, waterfront apartment with Egyptian cotton towels, not with the cheapest paper towels money could buy in a cell that stank of sweat and piss. *Who's got the better life*?

She grabbed the other Anna Mallory and slapped cuffs on her, leading her from the cell. As she did so, the woman said something that would haunt Commander Mallory for the rest of the day.

"*I* have," she said. "I've got the better life."

Chapter Thirteen

RAJ LANDED ON his side in one of the busiest shopping streets in Liverpool and nobody noticed. The absurdity of the situation didn't escape him. A man and a large dog appeared out of nowhere in the middle of the day and people just walked by glued to their phones. One suited city-type even stepped over Raj's legs without missing a beat, no doubt thinking he was a drunk or one of the homeless beggars who used to be everywhere before they were purged from the streets.

It suited Raj; he didn't want to attract attention. Placing one hand on Misha's back for support, he battled the nausea and got to his feet. The dog just stood there, happily wafting her tail in his face. It was a curious thing; Raj had jumped with Misha several times, and even though it always turned his guts inside out, it never bothered her.

Now he was on his feet, Raj had to decide what to do next. He felt weak and cowardly for fleeing from the horrific scene at the Foundation, and briefly considered going back, but there were plenty of good people left who were more than capable of dealing with it and Remick had been so insistent that he got out.

Clearly, Remick thought Raj was better employed elsewhere, but where and for what purpose? Things were spiralling out of control, and Raj had no idea what to do, but at least there was one thing he didn't have to worry about: Joey wasn't left behind. If Davina was right, and Joey had disappeared before the trouble started, all Raj had to figure out was where the hell Joey had got to and what he was doing. He wasn't sure which prospect worried him more. Then it came to him in a flash. He knew where Joey had gone.

"That's it, Misha! Come on, girl. You've never been to London, have you?"

Misha gave him one of her impenetrable looks, the looks Raj always took to mean she was humouring him. But it made sense. London was at the heart of everything, or more precisely, the site of the disaster at Trafalgar Square. Assuming Remick was correct, Saunders' arrival on this world had caused the disaster, and it was very likely Saunders was behind the psychotic seabirds.

Go to London, find Joey, stop Saunders, job done. Raj called Misha to heel and set off in the direction of Lime Street station. Just how one of the country's most wanted and his very recognisable dog, who wasn't on a lead, were supposed to get on a train then casually stroll into a high-security disaster site was something he would have to work out on the way. He remedied a small part of the problem by picking up a length of rope he spotted in an alleyway and tying it to his companion's collar. Misha chuffed a half-hearted protest but allowed him to do it and walked obediently by his side as if it were her usual lead.

It was only when Raj started to climb the stone steps up to the station entrance that he discovered his problems were rather more complicated than he'd first thought. In his haste to leave his quarters, he'd snatched up his jacket, but his wallet was where he always left it: on his bedside table. He didn't have enough loose change in his pocket for a cup of coffee, let alone the fare to London. It was risky enough making the trip, but to try and dodge the fare as well was suicidal. Not only that, but he'd also left his mobile behind.

He was faced with a relatively simple choice: go back for his wallet and phone and face getting caught up in whatever was going on at the Foundation, or...find another way. Jumping was out of the question. He'd never gone that far before and had no idea if he even could. The only time he'd jumped more than a short distance, he'd done it with Remick's help, which was no longer available. He stood on the station steps with his dog by his side and no plan whatsoever.

***

Liza Hunt was completely unaware of the chaos she was about to face as she escorted the prisoner who had once been her colleague up in the lift. Billy Radley was pinned face-first against the lift wall by Dev Rees on one side and Lily Park on the other. Liza was poised to step in if he tried to break free of either of them and she was in a sufficiently bad mood to go in hard if she needed to. She'd trusted Radley. She could not, in all honesty, say she liked him, but they'd been on enough operations together for her to trust him to have her back. It was rare for anyone in the Foundation to betray them, but when it was someone she'd worked with so closely, it just made the betrayal worse and she wanted to hit him hard and go on hitting him.

As the lift eased to a stop, Liza knew immediately that something was badly wrong. From the other side of the doors she could hear shouts and the sound of running feet.

"Keep him here," she said to Lily and Dev. "Let me just see what's going on."

She opened the doors, and as she did so, the biggest black-backed gull she had ever seen tried to fly into the lift. She hammered on the button and the doors slid over, trapping the bird across its chest, one wing in and one out. The gull struggled and spat, pecking and snatching at thin air.

"Jesus!" Liza cried. "Do something! It'll get in!"

Dev let go of Radley and quickly grabbed the gull by its neck, avoiding its frantic beak, and twisted. There was a sickening snap, and the bird slumped where it was. Liza opened the doors again and the bird dropped to the floor with a muffled thump.

Outside, the air was filled with screaming gulls, and the corridor echoed with the yells of people trying to run away and striking out at the birds with any object that came to hand. The walls were streaked with gull guano and blood, and Liza could see several people lying lifeless on the floor. One man, whom Liza thought was called Alan and worked in admin, lay on the ground, trying to cover his face, while a gull repeatedly pecked at him with a red-smeared beak. The scene was one of utter carnage, and Liza froze in horror for several seconds before her instincts took over.

"Dev, watch him." She pointed to the strangely compliant Radley who was still pinned against the lift wall. "Lily, with me."

"Where to?"

"To find Raj or Davina. Preferably both. Someone needs to get a grip on this."

The lift doors slid shut and, with Lily right behind her, Liza ran in the direction of Raj's quarters, batting away attacking birds. By the time she reached the end of the corridor, one sleeve of her jacket was in rags, but thankfully her skin was intact.

The corridor that housed Raj's quarters was empty, but the sight that greeted Liza made her stop in her tracks so abruptly Lily nearly ran into her from behind. Then Lily saw, too, and turned away retching. There was something that may have once been a person on the floor. All that was left was a pile of tatters covering a skeleton virtually stripped of flesh and lying in a slick of viscous, near-black blood.

"Oh, shit," Lily gasped. "That's not…"

"I hope not. Not Raj. We need to find Davina. Now!"

Behind them, they heard footsteps, and a young man whom Liza thought might be called Wallman staggered around the corner. He was holding one arm, and the sleeve of his shirt was sodden with blood from a wound in his bicep. His eyes were wild with fear and confusion.

"Liza! Thank God! What the hell is all this? Those birds…"

"Where's Davina?" Liza demanded. "Have you seen her?"

"I don't know…I think so. Back there somewhere."

"What about Raj? Is he here?"

"Raj!" Wallman laughed bitterly. "He legged it when all this started. Left his mate behind, though."

"Then he's okay?"

"If he is, he's the only one." With that, Wallman limped away out of sight.

"Lily," Liza said as they both briskly set off back the way they'd come. "Find Davina. Tell her I'll be back. I need to get Raj."

"Didn't you hear?" Lily said. "He's left us."

"Raj wouldn't do that. That's why I need to find him."

The corridor that contained the lift was quiet now. For some reason, the gulls had ceased their attack. One or two were just standing there, like troops awaiting orders. Further along, two of the birds squabbled over the prone body of a woman who hadn't survived the attack. Then, as if a silent command passed between them, they took off almost as one, flew out through the broken window and dispersed into the sky. The silence following their departure was broken by the distant cries of the injured, and Liza was torn between going to help and trying to locate Raj. There would be plenty of people to assist the wounded, so she hit the button to call the lift.

"Go on, Lily," she said. "Davina's going to need you. I've got to do this."

The lift chimed and the doors parted. Liza was about to step inside, when Lily stopped her.

"Where's Dev? He was in there with Billy."

***

Devon Rees was face-down on the floor of the car park, his eyes open but unseeing. Billy Radley stood nearby, muttering under his breath in reply to the voice in his head.

He wished it had been that Hunt bitch in the lift with him, but while his forehead was pressed up against the wall of the lift with Rees's shoulder in his back, he'd heard the voice again—the one that had promised him fame and recognition and was now giving him other instructions. He'd waited until the lift had begun to move, then placed both his hands on the wall and shoved violently backwards. Rees had stumbled over his own feet and Billy had shaken free of his grip. He'd managed to get both hands around Rees's neck, squeezing with a strength he had never felt before.

Rees had struggled at first, but by the time they reached the car park, the struggling ceased, and the lift filled with a foul stench as Devon Rees suffered the ultimate indignity of soiling himself as the breath and life ebbed from his body. The lift came to a stop, and Billy grabbed the front of Rees's shirt, hauled his corpse through the open door and dumped it on the ground. As soon as he stepped away and started to hear the voice again, Billy had forgotten Rees ever existed.

"*That was good,*" the voice was saying. "*You did well. He won't ever laugh at you again. Now, come to me, Billy.*"

"But I don't know where you are," Billy muttered.

"*I'll bring you. Concentrate.*"

"What about Chowdhury? And Hunt? You said I'd make them pay. You promised."

"*Don't whine. It's pathetic. Come to me now and you will have the power to make them all pay.*"

"I don't know. You said—"

"*Do you want me to give the power to someone else? I can, Billy. I can give it to anyone I want. I could give it to Hunt. Or Chowdhury. Do you want me to do that?*"

"No, I don't. But—"

"*They won't leave you alive, Billy, you know that, don't you? Not with the power I have to give. They would crush you and not give it another thought. It's your choice.*"

"But I don't know what to do!"

"*Concentrate. I will do the rest.*"

Billy tried to concentrate, to focus on his rage and resentment. As he did so, he could smell something burning, like a burger left for too long on the grill. He felt a tug at his core, and the car park in front of him faded from his vision. He screamed as every fibre of his being was torn apart.

The scream echoed and then the car park was empty apart from the broken corpse of Devon Rees, staring at nothing.

***

The burning smell was stronger, and Billy retched but brought up nothing but bitter-tasting bile. He spat it out and pulled up onto his hands and knees. His head felt like some of the worst hangovers he had ever experienced, and he couldn't get his bearings. He was somewhere dark, but just in front of him was what looked to be the remains of a fire casting a flickering red glow onto the ground. He must have been in a worse state than he thought, because as he watched, the embers moved and something began to rise from them. Billy stared in horror and disbelief as the figure of something like a man hauled itself out of the fire until it was standing more or less upright.

"*Billy,*" it said in a voice out of a nightmare. "*Welcome.*"

"What…?" Billy began, but he wasn't even sure what question he was going to ask.

"*No time for that,*" the thing, whatever it was, said. "*Come closer.*"

Billy was unable to resist and crawled closer to the fire. Suddenly something hit him in the mind like a hammer blow and his head was full of images, faces, a book of some kind, and he *knew.*

"Master," he said and knelt on one knee, his head bowed.

"*Enough of that,*" the thing that sometimes called itself Saunders said. "*Get up. You look ridiculous. Now, I need you to go somewhere.*"

"Chowdhury," Billy said. "You said—"

"*All in good time. I need to go and help a friend of mine first. Don't worry. I'm sure we can find you someone to kill.*"

Chapter Fourteen

THIS NEEDS TO be done in sterile conditions. It's a bit too important to do in the field."

Carla Lockhart was on her mobile and raging when Marianne reached the area which had hastily been set aside for their operations—a section of Charing Cross station main concourse which had been screened off with plastic sheeting. Where the concourse had, at one time, teemed with commuters and shoppers, it was now off-limits to the public and deserted apart from Lockhart and her team, and members of the various emergency services and investigation teams. Lockhart was standing next to the block of compacted clay, which was still on its gurney, and she wasn't in the least bit happy about it.

"No," she said, "we can't do anything with it here. ... You have no idea what you're dealing with, do you? ... You want I should explain, then? Whatever this is, it has been preserved in the wall for God knows how long. It has not been exposed to air, nor to pollution. The degradation of these bones started the second we took it out of there and— ... No, I'm not ready for you to bring your healer in. Don't be ridiculous. ... What? You wouldn't dare! ... Right. Fine. But it's on your head."

She slammed her phone down on the workbench and stared at it. "Bastard!" she hissed. "The complete, total, useless bastard."

"Problem?" Marianne asked.

"Martin goddamn Buxton. Told me they want to bring their miracle worker in now. When I told him...well, you heard what I told him, he suggested they might want to take a look at whether they can afford me or whether to bring in 'someone local', as he called it. He wants results, and he wants them now."

"So what are you going to do?"

"I'm going to start having a look at our bony pal here, right where we are, without the proper equipment or the proper conditions. And if what is potentially the most important archaeological find of this century is ruined by doing so, then the responsibility is squarely on Mr. Buxton's shoulders. Kyle and Nathan have gone back to the museum." Lockhart scribbled some notes on a pad, tore off the sheet and handed it to Marianne. "Give Nath a ring and tell him to get his butt down here and bring this all back with him. It's not enough but it will be a help."

While Marianne rang Lockhart's orders through, the archaeologist kitted herself out in a plastic coverall from a rail, took a new scalpel from a pack on the workbench and tore off its wrapping.

"Right," she said. "Let's have a look at you."

She bent low over the block of clay on the gurney and called over her shoulder to Marianne, "If you're done with that call, get yourself suited up and get over here."

***

Marianne took a coverall off the rail and climbed into it, hating the way these things always made her look like a giant, plastic-covered baby. She noticed there were three other coveralls still on the rail and wondered whether she could sneak a couple of them out before Nathan and Kyle got back. She took one, folded it as small as she could and stuffed it down the front of her own suit.

"Come on!" Lockhart called.

"Won't be a minute."

Hurriedly, she folded up and concealed another suit and, hoping it wouldn't show, zipped up her coverall and went over to where her superior was hunched over the gurney.

Lockhart was carefully cutting with the scalpel around one of the bones of the skeleton's arm, her face fierce with concentration. When she had finished cutting, she gave it a tug with a pair of tweezers, and it came free from the clay. She selected a soft brush from the bench and gently brushed the bone down. As the clay fell away, she frowned.

"Now I didn't expect that," she said. "Marianne, take a look."

"What am I looking at…oh. That's—"

"Weird. That's what it is. It's hollow and there's only half of it." Lockhart returned to the clay and scraped with the scalpel in the cavity where the bone had been. "Nothing," she said. "The other half of the bone isn't there. It's like…I don't actually know what it's like. I've never seen anything like that before."

"It's like a crab shell," Marianne suggested. "You know, when you think you've found a crab on the beach, but it isn't, it's just the shell."

"We need to get some more out. See what they're like. If it's only one, then it's some sort of freak thing, but if they are all like that…"

"What would it mean? I don't get it."

"It would mean we haven't found a skeleton at all. Your crab shell idea might be pretty close. It could be some sort of…well, I guess *exoskeleton* would be the best way to describe it. If that's the case, then we have discovered something nobody has ever seen before. I mean, have you ever heard of any creature that has a human-size exoskeleton and wings? Look, go see if those two slackers are on their way but *don't* tell them yet. This has to stay between the four of us."

Marianne nodded and went to go.

"I'll tell you one thing," Lockhart said, turning her attention back to the clay. "There's no way Buxton's witch-woman is getting anywhere near this."

***

"Angels. Really?" Emma said. She and Joey were huddled in a space at the bottom of the rickety staircase, keeping low and out of sight. So far, nobody had come down, but every creak of the stairs made them start.

"Well, if Saunders and Remick are demons, why not?"

"I can't believe you're so calm about all this. The thought of it freaks me out. I never even went to church, but the idea of demons and angels is just a bit much."

"You saw Saunders. You saw what he can do."

"Yeah, he killed me. Thanks for the reminder."

Joey put his arm around Emma's shoulders. He didn't even think about it; it just seemed the right thing to do. "He won't do it again."

"You see? How mad does that sound? We're talking about a demon killing me *again*. As far as I knew, it could only happen the once."

"I wish it hadn't. I wish I'd been able to stop it."

"But I'm here now. And now there's two of me in here, I feel like I'm better than ever."

"That must be so strange. Two of you. I can't imagine it."

"I don't even really think about it. I just...*am*. Do you know what I mean?"

"Not really. But I don't think I want to find out. How did you get back, though? How did you get here? You never said."

Emma laughed. It was a good sound, but out of place here. "I followed you, Joey. You kissed me, didn't you? When I was, you know..."

Joey turned his face away. "I thought you were dead."

"Hey, it's okay! I knew you had, though. Don't ask me how I knew because I can't explain it. Just like I can't explain how, when I heard that heartbeat, I knew it was yours."

"What heartbeat?"

"Told you I couldn't explain it. When I was dead, I could hear this heartbeat, and I followed it. It led me here. You've got a very strong heartbeat, Joey. I don't think you're going to have a heart attack anytime soon."

"It's damaged, my heart, although I got off lightly. The Joey on this world didn't make it."

"Poor thing. That's something else I can't get my head around—this whole other worlds thing. I wonder how many there are. I wonder how many of us there are out there and if they've met each other."

"Who knows? I'd just be happy to get back to the world I came from. I try not to think about my parents too much, but I miss them. God knows what's going through their minds. I don't even know how long I've been missing now."

"I should try and contact Emma's mum—*my* mum, whatever—but I don't know if the Green Jackets will have been there looking for me. Not that she'll have noticed I've gone."

"Once we're out of here, you can ring her."

"Yeah." Emma snorted. "Once we're out of here."

"We will. That woman, Marianne, she'll help. At least we know she's on the right side."

"If she is. I'm starting to wonder if anyone is who they say they are."

Joey felt for Emma's hand in the gloom. She didn't respond at first, but he gave it a squeeze and she curled her fingers around his.

"We'll be okay," he said. "We'll get out of this."

He was suddenly all too aware of how close her face was to his, and her breath on his skin. He wondered what it would be like to kiss her while she was actually conscious. He was just about to take a chance and find out when there was a clang above their heads, followed by the unmistakable sound of footsteps coming down the stairs. They shrank back, trying to get as far into the space under the stairs as they could. Joey felt Emma tense up, aware she was holding her breath, and he was doing the same. The footsteps continued down the stairs and then stopped with a crunch at the bottom.

"You there?" Marianne whispered.

Joey held Emma back and emerged on his own from hiding. "Are you on your own?"

"Of course I am," Marianne replied testily. "Did you think I was going to bring everyone with me?"

"No, sorry. Just being careful."

"Fair enough. But you've got to get out of here now." She reached into the front of her coverall and pulled out two crumpled suits. She handed one to Joey and the other to Emma, who had come out from under the stairs when she heard Marianne's voice. "Put these on and I'll take you up. Keep your hoods up and your heads down and get out as fast as you can."

Joey and Emma fumbled their way into the plastic suits and pulled the hoods over their heads.

"I feel stupid," Emma said.

"You look it," Marianne replied. "But it's better than being caught. I'm going to talk to you like you're colleagues, okay? But don't reply. Just nod or whatever, and leave the talking to me. Now, come on. Let's move."

Marianne started off up the stairs, with Emma following and Joey bringing up the rear. When they were halfway up, Marianne began to speak.

"Yes, so the thing is, Lockhart's on the warpath now. Like, we're stuck here when we could be doing all this back at the museum, and she's hell-bent on finding out what that thing is and getting all the glory. I mean, it was bad enough when she thought it was a skeleton. Now she's figured out it's more like an exoskeleton, she's going nuts about it."

They reached the top of the stairs, and Joey and Emma found themselves in part of a deserted train station, but it was one that looked like part of a war zone. The tiles on the walls were cracked and scorched, and part of a coffee shop nearby had collapsed in on itself. Two men in hi-vis jackets were approaching, and Marianne started to talk louder.

"The sooner we're done here the better. This place creeps me out. And now they want to bring that bloody healer woman in. I mean, what's that all about?"

The two men passed out of earshot and went down the steps. Joey stopped walking.

"Wait. *What* did you just say?"

"I said don't talk," Marianne hissed. "It's not hard."

"You said healer woman. What healer woman?"

"You don't need to know. I was just talking for talking's sake. Come *on*!"

"No, you weren't," Joey said. Emma shook her head and gave him a look. "We know more than you think. What's this healer woman's name?"

"They didn't—"

"Is it Anna? Is that her name?"

He could see realisation beginning to dawn on Emma's face.

"We know her. If it's Anna, she's a friend of ours. Look, if you're with the Catesbys, do you know Raj?"

"Raj Chowdhury? I know *of* him. But how do you know—"

"You need to get a message to Raj. Tell him about Anna. And if they're bringing her here, we have to stay. We're not leaving here without Anna."

Chapter Fifteen

THERE WERE TIMES when Richard Wells felt he wasn't taken seriously enough. When he had agreed to head up the Select Committee, he did it on the understanding the investigating team would report to him, and he, in turn, would report their findings to the Home Secretary and, by extension, the Cabinet and the Prime Minister. From the start, he had suspected he was nothing more than a figurehead, someone to talk to the press and possibly a scapegoat if the investigation went wrong or carried on too long. In one of their early meetings, he had raised the issue with the Home Secretary herself.

"Not at all, Richard," she had said. "Your role will be a vital one. It is essential those responsible for this atrocity are found and brought to justice. The public need to know the right person is overseeing this investigation, and with your record, you are clearly that person."

Wells knew his background was hard to argue with. Harrow followed by Sandhurst and two tours of duty in Afghanistan provided a solid basis for someone tasked with the biggest anti-terrorist investigation the country had seen. The fact Wells would still have been serving in the Royal Marines had a shell not nearly taken his leg off certainly helped his case, and his well-publicised campaign to be elected as an MP because he wanted to carry on serving his country, even if he could no longer fight, made him the darling of the media. He had easily won what had previously been considered a safe seat held by the esteemed opposition for just about as long as their party had existed.

This victory had meant he had risen and risen fast. Immediately after the Trafalgar Square attack, the name of Richard Wells was spoken of frequently as the person most likely to be brought in as the public face of the investigation. It was Wells who had insisted on Martin Buxton as the chief investigating officer. These days, however, it seemed Buxton reported directly to the Home Secretary and Wells was now simply the figurehead he had feared he would be all along.

It was for this reason Wells had requested another meeting with the Home Secretary and was now sitting across a table from her in a very exclusive members' club. The irony wasn't lost on either of them that, were it not for the Home Secretary's position, her gender would have made it highly unlikely she would ever have seen the inside of this particular club at all. Wells nursed a twenty-year aged scotch while the Home Secretary seemed content with mineral water.

"I'm curious to know why you have requested this meeting," she began. "Surely you and I would make better use of our time by simply getting on with our jobs."

"That's precisely my point," Wells answered. "I don't feel like I am being permitted to do my job."

"And who, exactly, do you feel is stopping you?"

"My job depends on information. I can only do it properly if I am privy to all the data the investigation is providing. I am more than aware Martin Buxton is bypassing me and speaking directly to you. I need to ask, Ma'am, is there information pertinent to this investigation that I am not being given?"

The Home Secretary put her drink down, leaned back in her chair and steepled her fingers together. "If that were the case, Richard, what makes you think I would tell you now?"

"It really depends on whether you have someone else lined up to replace me."

"Are you threatening to resign? That's a little childish, don't you think?"

"Not at all. If I am the public face of this whole thing, then you owe it to me not to let me make a fool of myself by withholding information. If you can't do that, then I'm afraid you really give me no choice."

"So what is this information you believe I am keeping from you?"

"The real purpose of the investigation. If Trafalgar Square was destroyed by terrorists or anarchists or whatever the hell we're telling the public this week, some evidence would have been found by now. I believe Buxton and his people are looking for something else down there and you know what it is."

"Really? And what do you think that might be?"

"I don't know, Ma'am. That's what I was hoping you might see fit to share with me."

As Wells was speaking, he was half-aware of a commotion behind him. One of the club stewards was arguing with someone at the door.

"I can tell you, Richard, that we are not looking for anything down there. We *were*, but not any longer. We have found what we were looking for." The Home Secretary was interrupted by the approach of the steward, who stood just behind her chair and cleared his throat.

"I'm sorry, Ma'am," he said. "I did explain that you were in a confidential meeting, but he was most insistent."

"That's fine, James. I was expecting him."

The person who had been arguing with the steward stepped into view, and Wells was alarmed to see a stocky, shaven-headed man in his thirties or thereabouts, with a livid-looking open wound on his forehead.

"Richard, let me introduce you to Mr. Radley. Mr. Radley has been working with our old friends the Catesby Foundation, but has now come to work for us. That thing we were just discussing—the thing we were looking for? Mr. Radley is going to retrieve it for us."

"Home Secretary, I don't understand! Why has this man been brought into this investigation without my knowledge? I really must protest!"

"You can protest all you like, Richard." The Home Secretary looked at him over the top of her glasses and smiled the patronising, insincere smile despised by television interviewers.

In that second, Wells thought he caught a flash of something red in her eye. "But it won't do you any good. You'll be pleased to know I accept your resignation, effective immediately. There is too much at stake here to tolerate anyone who is not completely loyal. My master has been waiting for this. We have been preparing for a very long time." She turned to the shaven-headed visitor, who had a hungry look in his eye that turned Richard Wells' stomach to ice. "Billy, would you be so good as to escort Mr. Wells from the premises? Our meeting is over."

Wells was about to protest, but the man called Billy laid a firm hand on his shoulder. Wells stood up and defiantly drained his glass.

"All right! I'm going. But don't think you've heard the last of this. I have contacts in the press—"

Before he could say any more, the Home Secretary's new associate seized his arm and steered him towards the door. As he went, he heard the Home Secretary talking in low, confidential tones to the club steward.

"—overdoing it a bit. I'm very concerned about him, actually. I think there may be trouble at home. My friend will make sure he is all right."

With these words echoing in his ears, Wells was manhandled down the marble-tiled hallway of the club and out through its immense carved-oak door. Once outside on the pavement, he tried to shake free of Billy Radley's grip.

"That's fine, thank you," he said. "I can see myself home from here."

"I'm sorry, Mr. Wells," came the reply as Radley propelled him towards an alleyway at the side of the club, "but I'm afraid you won't be going home."

Chapter Sixteen

NATHAN WILDE WAS having the sort of day nobody warned you about while you were studying for an archaeology degree. They told you that you might spend endless days digging about in freezing cold fields and finding nothing. They warned you that you might never find that object of massive historical importance that you always dreamed of uncovering. They warned you that dressing in a leather jacket and hat and carrying a whip would prevent anyone from taking you seriously. They did not, however, warn you that one day you would be standing at a makeshift workbench in the ruins of an abandoned railway station examining the strangest book you had ever seen in your life.

At first glance, the book looked normal enough. Antiquarian bookshops were full of books just like it—large, grimy leather-bound tomes with foxing on the pages caused by age and damp. But there were several things about this particular book which caused Nathan some confusion.

First of all, it was locked. Across the opening edge was a leather strap, fastened with a rusted metal snap, which gave it the appearance of a large, old version of a teenager's diary. He had made a tentative effort to open the fastener, but it refused to move, and the presence of a keyhole and the absence of a key meant he was unable to open it without forcing or picking the lock, neither of which he was prepared to try without Carla Lockhart's express permission. The risk of breaking it was too great.

The second thing that confused Nathan was the condition of the book. Yes, it was pretty worn and dirty, but no more than you might expect from a book that old. It could have been taken from the shelf of an antique shop yesterday; it certainly didn't look like it had been buried in a clay wall for however long. The edges of the pages should have felt damp and been wrinkled with moisture, but from what Nathan could see under the cover, the paper was dry.

The thing that confused him most, though, was the leather cover itself. It felt like no leather he had come across. It had a slightly clammy texture, which was unpleasant to the touch and reminded him of the skin of an uncooked chicken. He wanted to try and take a sample and examine it under one of the microscopes he and Kyle had brought over from the museum, but again, he would need to ask Ms. Lockhart before he did anything like that. She was rather preoccupied at the moment, deep in conversation with Marianne Bond on the other side of their temporary workshop. He thought about getting another opinion from Kyle, but his colleague was fiddling around with some of the equipment they had brought and looked like he was concentrating hard.

Instead, Nathan turned his attention back to the lock. Earlier, he had squirted some lubricant into it and left it to soak, just in case it had simply seized up with rust. He placed the tip of his finger on the lock and tried to move it, but the lock was still tight and unmoving. He selected a small wire brush and cautiously tried to brush away some of the corrosion, but that made no difference either.

He placed the book back on the workbench and, without any real idea what he was looking for or much hope of success, opened a browser on his phone and tried researching similar books on a few antiquarian book sites. As he did so, he heard a faint click from the workbench. He glanced up from his phone and saw that somehow the catch on the book's lock had sprung open. He looked over at Carla Lockhart, but she was still talking to Marianne, so, without seeking further approval, he slipped on a pair of disposable latex gloves and opened the book's cover.

***

"I'm not sure how you think we're going to manage it," Marianne said. Carla Lockhart's suggestion would have been outrageous at the best of times, but right now, it was in danger of derailing her plans altogether. "We can't just stick it under our coats and smuggle it out of here."

"I'm hoping we don't have to. But I'm not prepared to work here any longer, and I'm *definitely* not prepared to have your government looking over my shoulder all the time."

"Not *my* government. I didn't vote for them."

"Well, I sure as hell didn't. We just need some kind of distraction—"

"Then what? Just wheel it out of here? The museum is a couple of miles away!"

"I think Kyle's got a van, hasn't he? Hey, Kyle!"

Kyle looked up from his work.

"You still got that beat-up old van of yours?"

Kyle nervously rubbed his beard, which was one of those scrubby, unconvincing beards that only the young believe look good. He always seemed jumpy when Carla Lockhart spoke to him, or indeed any woman.

"Yes, I have, Ms. Lockhart," he replied, sounding for all the world like the teacher had asked him if he had done his homework.

"You come in it today?"

"No, sorry. I came by bike. Why?"

"Never mind. Keep up the good work."

Kyle flushed bright red and bent his head back over the workbench.

"I swear that boy is going to faint every time I talk to him," Lockhart said to Marianne with a grin.

"He probably fancies you."

"The boy couldn't handle me. And he's no damn help either. Can't shift that thing on a bike."

Marianne didn't reply. Somewhere on the other side of the plastic sheeting that made a vague pretence at privacy for the archaeologists' work, Joey Cale and Emma Winrush were concealing themselves, refusing to leave, determined to rescue this healer woman. They were in danger of exposing Marianne and there wasn't a thing she could do about it until she could get away from Lockhart and make a call to alert the Foundation. Before she could even think about how to answer, however, Nathan started screaming and all hell broke loose.

***

The first thing Nathan noticed when he opened the book was that the words written inside were in English, and modern English at that, which, considering the age of the book, didn't make much sense. The second thing he noticed was what was written in the book. At first, he interpreted them as fictional stories, all of them set in the present day, which, for a book that had been buried for so long, simply could not be possible. Nathan started to read the first story he came to when he randomly opened the book, about a man being tormented by a mysterious figure in a wood yard opposite his house, and suddenly his head flooded with stories. He could see them as vividly as if they were happening right in front of him.

There was a man who was given a tankard which had a handle made out of the Horn of Plenty and drank himself to death. There was someone who found an old school photograph, on which the faces of everyone who had died since the photo was taken had vanished. There was a writer who lost the use of his hands in a mugging, a man who wanted to rid his garden of snails but fell victim to the snails' revenge, a masked ball where, under their masks, nobody had a face—so many stories Nathan's brain couldn't take them all in and they were all happening at the same time and they were all true. Nathan's mind couldn't process all the stories bombarding it and he screamed. He dropped the book but hit the floor before it did.

***

Marianne heard the scream and came running just as Nathan fell to the ground.

"Nathan!" she yelled, and then, "Someone get an ambulance!"

She knelt down beside her young colleague and felt his wrist for a pulse. It was there, but weak. Nathan's face had gone slack on one side, and one end of his mouth was dragged down, a thin trickle of saliva running from it. She looked up to see Carla and Kyle staring at her, not moving.

"Get a bloody ambulance!" she shouted again. "I think he's had a stroke!"

Chapter Seventeen

RAJ WAS BEGINNING to regret getting into the car, which was now speeding down the motorway in the direction of London.

He'd seen it, of course. Raj seemed to spend half his life watching vehicles as they passed him by, looking for the telltale slicked hair and sunglasses which would tell him he needed to run. So he'd noticed the orange VW Beetle straight away—it was difficult to miss on a road full of uniform silver and black cars—but he'd thought nothing much of it the first time, apart from a quick *who'd drive a car like that?*

At that point, he'd still been standing with Misha on the steps of Lime Street station, feeling exposed but undecided as to where to go, and this feeling of vulnerability made him watch the traffic even more closely than usual. However, it was only when the orange Beetle made a circuit of the block and drove past him again that he began to get suspicious. The sun glinted off the windows, so he couldn't get a good look at the driver, but it didn't seem like the kind of car Green Jackets would be seen dead in, unless they were working under deep and faintly ridiculous cover.

All the same, he looked around and plotted his best escape route, torn between running up the steps and into the station—which brought back painful memories of what had happened to the Raj Chowdhury of this world—or taking his chances with crossing the road against the traffic.

The third time he saw the Beetle, it was too suspicious to ignore, especially when it slowed down right beside him. He took tight hold of Misha's makeshift lead and prepared to flee, but then the window of the Beetle wound down and the very familiar voice of Liza Hunt called out, "Get in, for Christ's sake. I don't want a ticket!"

Raj had squeezed Misha uncomfortably into the back seat while he sat in the passenger seat with his knees nearly up to his chin, and Liza had taken off like a rocket before Raj could figure out how to fasten the seat belt. A bus had to slow down to let her out, and the driver sounded the horn angrily. It was when Liza swore in reply that Raj knew he was in trouble.

"Where did you get the car?" he asked. "Not your usual."

"Commandeered it. Well, stole it, really. That's why I didn't want a ticket. Why did you leave us?"

"You *stole* it? Jesus, Liza, what for? What if it's been reported?"

"I needed to leave in a hurry. Just like you did. I needed to find you. And you haven't answered me, Raj, Why did you leave? Have you any idea what went on back there? Those birds… They were killing people and you ran away. And Billy Radley—"

"What about Billy? What's happened?"

"I *told* you. I think he's gone mad. He tried to kill me. That's why I got you to send Lily Park and Dev Rees down. He *did* kill Dev."

"Dev's dead?"

"Billy strangled him. Now he's vanished. Just like you did. You've missed quite a lot, Raj."

"I didn't vanish. Remick told me to get out of there. I didn't have a choice."

"Remick? Who the hell is… Oh, wait a minute. Isn't that one of—"

"The hot codes? Yes. And with good reason. Remick was with us on the other world. He helped us then and tried to help us now, but those birds took him apart, Liza. I've never seen anything like it."

"I have. Because they didn't stop, Raj. They might have come for your mate, but they didn't stop. What made them do that? It's not normal."

"I don't think you could call anything about this normal. Remick said it was *him*—Saunders. He said Saunders could possess lesser species."

"Oh, yeah. Saunders, the other demon. I heard the stories." Liza had a note of cynicism in her voice. "Where are we going, by the way? Or are we just driving around waiting for someone to notice?"

"London."

"*London*? What the hell for?"

"Because I'm pretty sure that's where Joey's gone. I'm also fairly sure that's where Saunders is. Remick said something about stopping him finding a book."

"A book? You want to go to London for a book? Couldn't we just go to Waterstones?"

"London's at the centre of everything. It's all connected to the attack on Trafalgar Square. And the stories are true, mostly."

"Yes, but demons, though. Really?"

"You had to be there. Have you got enough petrol in this thing?"

***

Relations between Raj and Liza remained tense for the first part of the journey, especially when Liza had to pay for the petrol when Raj confessed to leaving his wallet behind. She complained about it off and on from Liverpool to Stoke-on-Trent. Eventually, though, as they put some distance between them and the horrors they had left behind, a thaw set in. By the time they reached the Cherwell Valley service station, with London nearly within reach, and decided to stop to get a coffee and let Misha stretch her legs, they were talking like old friends again. Raj could only hope it would continue once Liza realised she would have to pay for the coffees too.

***

While Raj exercised Misha, Liza headed off to find the toilets and freshen up. Just the thought of it reminded her how desperate she was, and she was in such a hurry she only vaguely paid attention to the two women who were leaving the ladies' as she entered. They were so alike they could be twins, and there was something vaguely familiar about them, but then the door closed and they were gone. Liza used one of the cubicles then washed her hands and face. Feeling much better, she went to find Raj.

It was while Raj was trying to coerce Misha back into the Beetle that Liza saw the two women again and got a better look at them. They were crossing the car park towards a black SUV with tinted windows. Both women had long, dark hair, but one had it pulled back in a neat, if severe, ponytail while the other one's hair could have done with a brush. One was dressed in a smart black pantsuit and leather coat, while the other looked like she had slept in her clothes. The neater of the two turned her head and gazed back at Liza, and Liza was again convinced she had seen the woman before.

"Look," she said, nudging Raj. "Those women."

"Bloody hell. That's Anna Mallory."

"What? Which one?"

"Both of them. Quick, back in the car. We need to follow them."

Chapter Eighteen

I'M SICK OF hiding," Emma said. "I want to do something."

"Like what?" Joey asked.

"I don't know. Something."

Even the tunnel had been a more attractive proposition for a hiding place than where they were. After they had refused to leave without Anna, Marianne had taken a call from her boss, who wanted to see her *right now*, and had ushered them, still wearing their coveralls, through a door off the concourse which turned out to be a now-disused public toilet. The lights only worked intermittently, and what they revealed when they came on made Emma wish they stayed off all the time. The tiles were cracked and covered in graffiti. A broken vending machine half hung off one wall, and the whole place was filthy. Not that they needed lights to see how dirty the room was; the smell told them all they needed to know. Marianne had promised to return as soon as she could, but as yet there was no sign and Emma was getting restless.

"We need to get Anna and get out of here."

"And go where? This isn't my world, Emma. It's only half yours, but I don't belong here."

"Have you given any thought to how you might get back?"

"Yes, I thought I'd find someone to shoot me in the chest and see what happens. There seems to be plenty of people with guns around. I might just get lucky."

"Hey, I thought I was the sarcastic one!"

"I've learned well. No, I have no idea how I'm going to get home. I doubt if I will. I think I'm probably stuck here."

"You'll be stuck here with me, if that's any consolation."

Joey smiled, but only weakly. "It's more being stuck here with Saunders that bothers me. I think we might have to deal with him."

"Then we'll deal with him. But we'll do it together. Let's see if we can sort Anna out and then maybe round up your mate Raj. The four of us nearly beat him last time and we didn't know what we were doing. This time, we can be a bit more prepared."

"But—"

"And don't say he killed me. It's old news and it didn't stick. But I'll tell you one thing, we're not going to do anything about any of it stuck in here. If Marianne doesn't get back in a minute, I say we go and look for her."

It was then that they heard the scream. It came from somewhere too close for comfort and echoed down the station concourse. Without a word, Joey and Emma left the ruin of the toilets at a run.

As they burst through the plastic sheeting which had been rigged up to shield the area, the place was in chaos. Marianne Bond was crouching over a young man who was lying prone on the floor; a woman with short dark hair was yelling into her phone and swearing in an American accent; another young man was just hanging around looking useless.

"I don't care!" the American woman shouted. "I've got a twenty-something kid here who's had a stroke and he needs an ambulance *now,* goddamnit! … No, I won't hold. If you can't help me, for Christ's sake get me someone who can!"

Emma squatted down next to Marianne. The young man on the floor was barely moving, and the sounds coming out of his mouth were just wet noises. His eyes were rolled back into his head, and the left side of his face was dragged down and had the colour and texture of damp modelling clay.

"What happened?" Emma asked.

"I don't know," Marianne replied. "He just screamed and collapsed. Looks like a stroke, but he's too young." She dropped her voice to a low hiss. "You can't be here. This place will be crawling with security any minute."

While this exchange was going on, Joey crouched nearby, looking at something on the floor. Then a furious American voice said, "And who the hell are you?" and both he and Emma shot to their feet. The woman looked them up and down, taking in their coveralls, for which Joey offered a silent vote of thanks to Marianne.

"We were just passing," Joey said hurriedly. "We're working down the way there, and we heard the scream."

"Well, unless you're first-aid trained or have a hotline to this country's shitty ambulance service, you can just go back the way you came."

"You can't talk to us like that," Emma protested. "Who do you think you are?"

"I think I'm in charge of this set-up, so I'll talk any way I damn well want. So unless you can help, off you go!"

Somewhere in the distance a siren began to wail.

Emma tugged Joey's sleeve. "We'd better shift," she said. "Don't want to get in the way."

"Hope your friend's okay," Joey said to Marianne, and he and Emma ducked out of the plastic sheeting. From up the corridor, they could hear the sound of hurrying feet and the crackling of radios. Joey and Emma dodged through the nearest doorway—back in the toilets again.

"Oh, great," Emma said. "Thought we'd seen the last of this place."

"We'll get out of here in a minute," Joey said, reaching into the front of his coveralls. "What do you make of this?"

He handed Emma the object he had pulled out.

"Where did you get this?"

"It was on the floor next to that guy."

"It's a book, Joey. Probably his bedtime reading. Feels old, though. It feels like…I don't really know, but I don't like it very much. What did you pick it up for?"

"I'm not sure. It called to me."

"It called? It's a book, Joey. Books don't call."

With a loud buzz, the lights came back on, and Emma looked at the book in her hands.

"It's an old, knackered book. Should be in a skip." She pulled back the catch, opened the cover and read what was printed in elaborate, copperplate writing on the first page. "*The Book of Reasons*? Who'd call a book that?"

"It's Saunders," Joey said, making Emma shut the book with a slap. He took it from her. "I can feel it. It's got his stink all over it."

***

In a cavern no more than a mile from where Joey and Emma were standing, but deep underground, Billy Radley, his hands still wet with the blood of Richard Wells, raised his head to look at his master. The smouldering, ash-encrusted remains of the thing that sometimes called itself Saunders swayed unsteadily, its eye sockets blazing with fire.

"*He has the book!*" it said. "*That boy has the book!*"

Something in the back of Billy's mind told him what he was witnessing was impossible—that a thing made of cinders and bone could not be living, could not be speaking—but his head was filled with flame and blood and he couldn't think straight. His master staggered nearer, and Billy felt the heat on his face, making his eyes water.

"*I need your shell,*" Saunders said and reached out a skeletal hand. Billy flinched as it touched his forehead, scorching the skin like a brand. He screamed until his throat was raw and there was no more air in his lungs. When the screaming was done, the two figures remained in a macabre tableau, a shaven-headed man kneeling before a skeleton made out of charcoal and charred bones. Then the skeleton, the fire now extinguished in its eye sockets, disintegrated, collapsing into a heap of ashes on the ground. The man who had once been Billy Radley, but would now be known by the name of Saunders, stood up.

"Not too bad," he said, inspecting this new body. "Good muscle tone. Short-sighted in the left eye. Liver borderline alcoholic and terrible lungs, but it will do."

His eyes blazed red, and his lips formed themselves into a grin.

"Now then, Joey Cale, you thieving little bastard. I want my book back."

Chapter Nineteen

RAJ AND LIZA followed the black SUV at a discreet distance, always staying two or three cars behind. Even so, Raj was amazed they were able to make it to London without anyone in the SUV noticing the orange Beetle behind them.

"Maybe it's because it's so—well—*orange*," Liza suggested. "Who's going to be stupid enough to follow them in a car that looks like this?"

All the same, they proceeded cautiously, half expecting to hear sirens behind them or to see the car up ahead try to elude them. But nothing happened, and it continued to happen all the way to London. As they were nearing the city limits, Raj asked to borrow Liza's mobile. She passed it over without taking her eyes off the road and even managed not to remark on the fact Raj didn't have his own phone. He found Davina Watson's number in the phone book and called it.

"Damn. Voicemail."

"Who? Davina?" Liza asked. "I'm not surprised. There's a hell of a mess to clean up back there. Try Lily Park."

Raj nodded and tried Lily's number.

"Lily? ... No, it's Raj. ... No, she's with me. I haven't got time to explain, but can you get a message to Davina for me? ... Yes, she's probably called me worse before. Just get a message to her please. Tell her we're mobile and en route for London. ... Yes, Lily, I know. Tell her to contact London branch. We might need backup. ... Just tell her, please. ... What? ... Yes, I'll pass it on. Thanks, Lily."

"What did she say?" Liza asked.

"She says she's going to kick your arse for running out on her. And to be careful."

"That sounds like Lily, all right. So what's the plan?"

"I haven't got one. We need to find out what they want with Anna and get her out of there if we can."

"Why? She's not our problem. She walked away, remember?"

"She had her reasons. But they won't have brought her here for nothing. I need to know why."

"What about your mate Joey?"

"He'll have to wait. One thing at a time. Hang on, they're going left. Don't lose them! Where the hell are they going?"

Liza swung the car down a left turn and followed the SUV as it skirted the main road and headed off into a residential area of Fulham. It made several more turns, then pulled off the road and through the entrance gates of an industrial estate. Liza stopped the car outside the gates.

"Can't follow them in there," she said. "They'd see us for sure."

"We'll have to go on foot, then," Raj said, flinging off his seat belt and getting out of the car. "Misha, stay! Good girl."

"Hey, wait a minute," Liza protested. "Get backup first."

"No time. I think Anna's in trouble. I need to get in there now. Coming?"

***

Anna had fought a rising wave of anxiety all the way to London. Nobody would say where they were going or what she was expected to do when they got there. She had just been hustled into the back of a car by the other Anna Mallory and two silent Green Jackets who made no attempt to conceal the guns they were carrying. One of the Green Jackets sat in the back with her, while the other one drove. Anna's evil twin, as she thought of her, sat in the passenger seat up front and spoke only to give directions to the driver.

Once on the motorway, there were very few directions to give, so most of the journey passed with nobody speaking at all. It gave

Anna far too much time to think, and the more she thought, the more anxious she became. They clearly wanted her for *something*, and the little demonstration she had been forced to do with the guard proved they wanted her for her healing abilities, but who she was expected to heal and why was something no-one was prepared to explain. She only hoped she could do it. She got the impression that her captors would not tolerate failure. If only she hadn't walked away from Raj and his organisation, then she wouldn't feel so alone.

The anxiety levels rose considerably when the other Anna ordered the driver to pull into a service station outside London. She insisted Anna accompany her inside for a toilet break, even though Anna tried to protest that she didn't actually need one. By the time they came out of the toilets, Anna's fears that everything could go drastically wrong had gone through the roof, and when, on the way back to the car, a young black woman looked at them with half-recognition on her face, Anna very nearly took her chances and made a run for it. But the other Anna kept such a firm grip on her arm she feared she might end up with permanent indentations on her bicep. Then it was back in the car and off again.

Anna had expected them to head straight into the middle of the city—she was sure she'd heard some mention of Canary Wharf—but the car drove through the gates of an industrial estate and stopped behind a disused printers', and she really began to fear the plans had been changed and she'd been brought here to be executed.

After ten minutes or so, Anna heard the sound of an engine, and a second black SUV pulled around the corner and parked up a few yards away from theirs. The other Anna nudged her and indicated she should get out of the car. Nervously, Anna did as she was told. Looking over her shoulder, she saw the Green Jackets get out of the car too, though they hung back, hands near their weapons.

The door to the other car opened, and a third Green Jacket got out, followed by a middle-aged woman, but it was only when the woman opened the rear door and ushered out its occupants that Anna understood just how much trouble she was in. They'd grown a little since she'd last seen them, and they looked bewildered and worried, but she would have recognised Evan and Ruby anywhere.

***

Raj and Liza also witnessed the children getting out of the car. Once the SUV had disappeared out of sight, Raj was all set to go charging into the industrial estate, until Liza insisted on caution and suggested they parked the Beetle a street away to make it less visible. Raj had agreed, but as soon as Liza stopped the car, he was off at something between a brisk walk and a jog, and she had to run to catch up.

"We need ground rules here," she said, standing in front of him and blocking his path. "We've got to do this properly."

"Yes, sure," Raj said, but he was already looking over her head towards the path the SUV had taken.

"My face is here," Liza said and then rolled her eyes. "I never thought I'd have to say that to you. No, seriously, Raj. Whatever happens, we do *not* engage. Is that clear?"

"Okay, fine."

"I mean it. We don't risk exposure and we don't engage. We wait for backup."

"Understood. Let's go."

Liza sighed and followed him down the path. When they reached the print works, Raj flattened himself against the wall and peered around the corner.

"Car's there," he said. "Looks like everyone's still in it."

"Now what?"

"We observe and we don't engage." Raj did a quick reccy and beckoned for Liza to follow him to a side door to the printers'. He tried the door and grinned.

"Not locked," he whispered. "Who'd have thought?"

Inside the print works, the air was cool and damp and smelled stale. Any machinery had been stripped out, but there were dusty papers lying around everywhere—old fliers, discarded posters, even a few wedding invitations for a ceremony that had taken place two years earlier. Raj and Liza picked their way through the debris as quietly as they could and crept over to a cracked window where, through the grime on the glass, they could just about see the SUV. Ducking down out of sight, they watched the second SUV pull up. The two Anna Mallorys got out of the first car, followed by two Green Jackets. Then they watched in horror as the occupants of the other car emerged. Raj swore so loudly Liza had to shush him.

"The kids," he said. "They've got the kids."

"What kids?"

"Ruby and Evan. The kids who came here with us. What the hell are they doing here?" He started to get up, but Liza roughly pushed him back down again.

"Stay here!" she hissed.

"They're just children!"

"And they're still alive. That's more than we'll be able to say about you if you show your face. Listen to me, Raj. You're too valuable. I can't let you risk arrest, or worse, for the sake of a couple of kids. You agreed not to engage. We stay here and watch, whatever. Please?"

"For now," Raj said.

***

Anna wanted to run to the kids but was more than aware that, with three armed Green Jackets lurking around, it was a risk that wasn't worth taking.

"Where's Joey?" Evan asked, looking anxiously up at the woman who had brought them. "Dr. Franklin, you said we'd see Joey."

"All in good time, Evan," Dr. Franklin said. "I thought you'd like to see another of your friends first."

"What are they doing here?" the Anna in the leather coat asked.

"I thought they told you. They've come along in case our friend here needs a bit of persuasion to cooperate. Orders from the Home Office no less."

"Let them go. They're only children."

"Going soft, Commander Mallory? That's not like you."

Suddenly a small voice said, "Evan?" and Franklin looked around to see the girl, Ruby, was standing there on her own.

"The boy!" Franklin said. "Where's the boy gone?"

Then everything went wrong.

***

From his vantage point by the window, Raj saw Evan disappear. He had never actually witnessed it before, but one second, Evan had been standing there, right next to his sister and the woman who had brought them here; the next, the air around him had blurred, and then Evan was gone. He heard the woman shout and saw the Green Jackets looking helplessly around. The one who had arrived with the woman and the children had drawn his gun and was about to make a move when Anna—his Anna—screamed "NO!" and ran, not at the Green Jacket but away from the cars.

Time seemed to freeze, apart from Anna's running footsteps. Raj didn't even have time to think about jumping before a loud crack ripped through the air. Outside, the Green Jacket stared disbelievingly at his still-smoking gun as the lifeless body of Anna Mallory was thrown forward by the bullet's impact and kicked up a cloud of dust as it hit the ground and slid to a stop.

Chapter Twenty

EMMA LEANED AGAINST a filthy, cracked sink watching Joey pace backwards and forwards in the confines of their toilet hideaway, the book in his hands.

"I don't see Saunders with a book," she said. "He didn't really strike me as the reading type."

"I reckon it was dug up somewhere down here. Those guys are archaeologists, right? That's why they had it. Saunders is somewhere down here. Every time I do the heart thing and end up somewhere, it always seems to be where he is. And Davina Watson said something came from somewhere else and hit Trafalgar Square. Saunders came from somewhere else. It all ties up, and it all comes back to him. He was in no fit state to move around when I saw him. He tried to get you to work for him, just like he did with Ruby last time. So who's working for him now?"

"You're making some big leaps here, Joey."

"You said the Green Jackets were set up because of Trafalgar Square. Davina said the same. What if they're *all* working for him? What for? What does he want? On the other world, he wanted freedom. He's got that, but what does he want now? He's gone to a hell of a lot of trouble."

"If you're right."

"I think I am. I think he's after something that will help him, maybe restore him somehow."

"And you think it's a book? I know they said at school that reading's good for you, but—"

"Wait a minute!" Joey stopped pacing and slapped himself on the forehead. "She *told* us! Marianne. She told us. Remember when she was telling us about the thing they found? What did she say?"

"She said it was a skeleton."

"No, she didn't. She said it *wasn't* a skeleton. It was an exoskeleton."

"What's the difference? Sorry, Joey, but I failed biology."

"Think about crabs or lobsters. Their shells protect them. It's like their skeletons are on the outside."

"Saunders isn't a crab, though."

"We don't know what he is. Not really. Think about it. He's down there. Some sort of, well, armour is probably the best thing to call it, has been found here. Someone who can heal is on the way. Put it together, Emma."

"Where does the book come in?"

"I don't know. Maybe it's the instruction manual."

"Shouldn't we look?"

"I don't know. It feels wrong." Joey paused and stared at the book in his hands. "Oh, hell, it's only a book," he said and opened the lock.

***

Terry Byrne and John Austin were on a routine patrol around the entrance drop-down to the tunnels. Both were constables on secondment from Thames Valley Police, and they were more used to walking the streets than patrolling around inside a bombed-out railway station, but you went where you were sent and got on with it. Since the flurry of activity when something had been found down there, the patrols had been pretty boring, but the overtime was useful.

"Jacqui wants a holiday," Byrne was saying as they walked. "I've got my eye on a Harley, but you know what they're like."

"At least you'll get a holiday out of it," Austin replied. "My one wants a new bathroom. I need a new car, but she wants a bleeding bathroom."

"They'll get what they want, though." Byrne laughed. "We do the bloody overtime and they get what they want."

They paused at the top of the staircase leading down to where the archaeologists had been working.

"Think we need to go down?" Austin asked.

"Nah. They're not here now. Anyway, I hate those stairs. Always feel like they're going to fall down."

Before they could move on, Byrne's radio crackled into life.

"Greyhound Seven, this is Trap One, are you receiving?"

"This is Seven," Byrne replied. "Receiving you. Go ahead, Trap One."

"Incident reported on concourse two. Ambulance called and on the way. Please attend."

"Understood, Trap One. Seven out."

"Concourse two?" Byrne said. "Isn't that where—"

John Austin wasn't paying attention. He was standing at the top of the staircase, looking down.

"John? Did you hear me?"

"Listen!" Austin said.

"We've got a shout, John."

"There's someone there!" Austin insisted.

Byrne listened and, sure enough, from down below came the clang of footsteps on the metal staircase. Byrne drew his baton and began to wish they were among the officers who had been trained with firearms.

"Who's there?" Austin called. "This is Constables Austin and Byrne. Identify yourself."

There was no reply, just the relentless sound of footsteps. In the darkness below, Austin saw two red dots glowing, like car brake lights in the fog.

"Stay where you are and identify yourself," Byrne called, joining his partner at the top of the stairs.

A figure emerged from the darkness—a man with a shaved head and…

His eyes! Look at his eyes! Byrne didn't have time to think anything more, because the man had reached the top of the stairs. He grabbed Byrne by the front of his jacket and spun around, hurling the officer down the stairs behind him.

"Don't come any closer," Austin warned, levelling his extended baton. "I'm warning you—"

The shaven-headed man took no notice of the warning and seized hold of Austin's baton, snapping it like a twig. He clamped a hand around Austin's throat and slammed him into the wall. As his head smacked into the tiles, Austin registered that maybe his wife wouldn't get her bathroom after all and then blackness took over.

The killer barely broke his stride as he tossed the officer's body aside like a pile of rags and carried on along the corridor.

***

The lock snapped open and Joey opened the book. He flicked through a few pages, then looked up.

"It's stories," he said. "What's Saunders doing looking for a storybook?"

"Maybe he needs some bedtime reading," Emma suggested. "Maybe he wants a hot milky drink too."

Joey looked down at the book again. "That's strange," he said. "It's different."

"I don't know that we have time for reading stories right now, Joey. You can have a nice sit down and a read later if you want."

"No, listen. I looked up, and when I looked back at the book, there was a different story on the page I was looking at. It's changed."

Emma sighed dramatically and went to the toilet door to listen.

"I don't know what's going on out there, but I wish they'd hurry up." Joey made no reply. "Joey, put the book down. I said..."

Emma glanced over at Joey, but he was just standing there, staring fixedly at the book. His face was pale and his whole body was trembling. She had no idea if he had ever had seizures—she still knew so little about him—but he was giving every appearance of having one now. She rushed over, not sure what she was supposed to do, and took hold of his arm.

"Joey? Joey, can you hear me?"

"The rabbit," Joey said, his lips barely moving. "The rabbit killed him."

The book's doing something to him.

A sharp pain in her hand distracted her momentarily; the squirrel bite was red and inflamed, which was strange. It was one of her other self's memories, and she'd more or less forgotten about it.

She ignored the stab of pain to concentrate on Joey. Taking hold of the book, she tried to wrestle it from his grasp, but his hands rigidly clung on, and she had to prise his fingers off it. Even when she had successfully pulled his left hand away and started working on the right, the left hand tried to snatch at the book again, and she slapped it away. A wave of pain from the squirrel bite made her gasp.

Again, she tried to blot it out, because Joey was shaking violently and had bitten his lip; a rivulet of blood ran down his chin. She managed to get two more of his fingers off the book and knocked it out of his hand with a hard, loud smack. The book skittered across the filthy, tiled floor and under a broken sink.

Joey stopped shaking immediately and looked at Emma, bewilderment in his eyes. Her hand throbbed, but she was so glad to see Joey back to something like normal she put it out of her mind and hugged him. He hugged her back, but it felt like a reflex.

"The rabbit killed him," he said again. He stepped back from Emma's embrace and shook his head like someone waking up from a dream. "What happened?"

"I think you nearly had a stroke too," Emma said. "It's that book. What the hell is it?"

"It's stories. So many stories. He's in them all."

"How can a book of stories do that? It doesn't make sense."

"There are too many stories to fit in the book so they go into your head instead. At least, I think that's what happens."

"That's insane. So what do we do with it now?"

"I'd say burn it, but I'm not sure it'll let you."

"*Let you*? It's a bloody book, Joey. It hasn't got a mind of its own."

"I think it has." Joey looked over at where the book lay on the floor. It seemed innocent enough.

Before he could say anything else, there was an ear-splitting crash from somewhere nearby, and the screaming started again.

Chapter Twenty-One

EVEN BEFORE THE dust had settled on Mallory's body, and before Liza could stop him, Raj vanished from inside the derelict printers' and reappeared outside. He picked up Anna's wrist and felt for a pulse. Finding none, he rounded on the Green Jacket, who was still standing there, gun levelled, unable to comprehend what he had just done.

"You killed her! She was unarmed and you shot her in the back!"

The mirror image of Anna, the commander in the leather coat, stepped forward and said to the Green Jacket, "Give me the gun."

The Green Jacket, obviously glad to be rid of it, handed the weapon over and took a pace back.

"Get in the car," Mallory said, gesturing with the gun and waving it at the two other Green Jackets. "I'll take responsibility for this mess. Get in the car with him." As they obeyed, she pointed at Dr. Franklin. "You too."

"But the children!" Franklin protested, her hands on their shoulders. Evan had reappeared as soon as he heard the shot and was straining to run to Anna.

"I'll take care of them. Get out of here, all of you."

Franklin and the Green Jackets climbed into the car. Mallory raised the gun and pointed it at Raj.

"You," she said loudly, "don't move a muscle. Get your hands in the air where I can see them and don't even think about disappearing. You're under arrest."

"Are you going to shoot me too?" Raj asked. "You want me to turn my back?"

"Just stay right where you are." Mallory had to raise her voice to be heard over the noise of the car starting up. She watched the SUV as it pulled out of the industrial estate, its tyres screaming. When it had gone, she lowered the gun. "You can put your hands down now."

"What, so you can murder me for trying to escape?"

"No, Raj." She tossed the gun onto the ground. "So I can give you a hug. I don't know about you, but I need one."

"What? I don't—"

"It's me, Raj. Anna. She made us swap clothes at the service station."

"This is a trick."

"It's not. I promise you."

"Prove it. What did I say to you in Liverpool the first time we met?"

"It wasn't in Liverpool. It was at Pendle. You were trying to save Joey, and you said something like, 'I don't know what you've got that I haven't, but go ahead.'"

"It was, 'Be my guest.'" Raj gazed at Anna for a moment, then hurried to her, wrapping his arms around her and hugging her long and hard.

"Careful," she said, eventually. "You want to get a reputation as a ladies' man?"

Raj let her go and beckoned to Ruby and Evan.

"It's okay, kids," he said. "It's Anna. Really."

The children looked uncertainly at each other, then rushed over. Anna picked Ruby up and Raj crouched down to hug Evan.

"He shot her!" Ruby cried.

"We thought it was you!" Evan joined in. "Why are you dressed like that?"

"Long story, mate," Anna said. "Don't worry. I'm fine. Better than I've been for a long time."

"It's a good question, though," said Raj. "Why *did* she do it?"

"I think she was just trying to distract them. She didn't explain why she wanted us to swap clothes and you don't argue with someone like her. I'm not sure what she was planning, but I don't think it was this. I'm guessing she wanted me and the kids to get away. Some sort of attack of conscience."

"I don't believe her sort *has* a conscience," Raj said, looking over at the body lying in the dirt.

"Do you think we should bury her?"

"I'm not sure anyone deserves to be left like that. But her mates are going to say something to someone, and it might just suit us if everyone thinks you're dead for now."

Any further discussion was ended by a voice from the window of the printers' behind them.

"Hey, Raj!" Liza called. "You know your dog's going mental in the car? Do you feel like telling me what the hell's going on?"

***

In the end, they thought it best to take the SUV and abandon the Beetle. Much as Liza had grown rather attached to it, fitting three adults, two children and a large dog into it was impractical and there were still a few miles to go to Trafalgar Square. Raj also argued that the Green Jackets were far less likely to pull one of their own vehicles over and it would make parking so much easier. In the end, Liza caved in and agreed.

"You haven't actually said what you're planning on doing when we get there," she said.

"Haven't a clue," Raj admitted. "I'll know when we get there."

"You mean you'll wing it as usual."

"Something like that, yes. Having the Commander of the Green Jackets with us will help us get in. *Then* we wing it."

"Er, Raj…" Anna said from the back seat. "Slight problem. Mallory left her mobile in her jacket. It's ringing."

"Then answer it," Raj replied. "But be careful. Remember who you are. Put it on loudspeaker."

"Okay," Anna said uncertainly and hit the answer key. "Mallory."

"Commander Mallory. Martin Buxton. Where are you, Commander? I was expecting you fifteen minutes ago. Is there a problem?"

"No problem, Mr. Buxton. Just traffic."

"And you have the woman with you?"

Anna caught Raj's eye in the rear-view mirror and made a *what do I say?* face. Raj nodded back.

"Yes, Mr. Buxton. Of course. Why do you ask?"

"No reason. I have the Home Secretary with me, and she's very keen to see our healer in action, as it were. I would hate to disappoint her."

"Mr. Buxton, I was instructed to drop everything and bring her and that is what I am doing. Now, was there anything else?"

"I'm not sure I appreciate your attitude, Commander."

"I'm sorry, Mr. Buxton. I seem to be losing the signal."

She severed the connection and, for good measure, switched the phone off completely.

"Creep," she said. "So what happens when we show up without Anna Mallory? What then?"

"We'll find out fairly soon," Liza answered. "We're nearly there. Get ready to start winging it, Raj."

***

Martin Buxton was still staring at his phone in outrage for a full minute after Mallory hung up on him.

"How dare she?" he demanded. "I'll have her job for this. Give me the authority and I'll have her giving out parking tickets."

Receiving no answer, he turned in his seat. The Home Secretary was sitting in the back of the government Mercedes, staring straight ahead. The car was parked just inside the security cordon that surrounded the shell of Charing Cross station.

"Home Secretary? Did you hear me? I said—"

"I heard you. I was speaking to someone rather more important."

"Speaking? I didn't hear—"

"Never mind. I want you to allow Anna Mallory and those with her to enter unimpeded."

"Why would they be impeded? I don't understand."

"Because your Commander Mallory is dead. The woman wearing her clothes is the healer. She will be accompanied by at least one person who is on a great many wanted lists, but they must be allowed to pass. Make sure all security personnel know this, Buxton. They will lead my master to the boy and to the book."

"Home Secretary, I need more information before I can give an order like that. What boy? And what book? I can't just—"

"You can and you will. You will have all the answers you require if you accompany me now. My master is about to rise and it will be glorious."

Any further words were drowned out by a deafening bang that made the ground beneath their feet shake and blew out half the remaining windows in what was left of the station. Martin Buxton stood there with his ears ringing and fragments of glass falling around him, and all he could think was *what the hell have I done?*

Chapter Twenty-Two

HENRY BEBB HAD been a paramedic for nearly twenty years and was heading rapidly for retirement. He had seen a great many things in those years. He had seen teenage boys lying in the street after being stabbed by someone who had been a friend just weeks ago. He had seen people who had managed to injure themselves in the most ridiculous and stupid ways, who could have saved a lot of time and resources by simply taking a bit more care. He had saved countless lives and been unable to save countless others.

He had been there just after the Trafalgar Square disaster and had worked for three days solid without sleeping, helping in the relief effort, ferrying survivors to overcrowded hospitals, never knowing who had lived and who had died. Every day, he arrived at work prepared to give his all, but every day was another one crossed off the calendar, another day closer to retirement and to the cottage in Yorkshire he was doing up, where he and his wife, Nicola, were going to see out the rest of their days.

For the last eight of those years, Henry had been partnered with Denise Howarth. Denise had been a raw recruit when she had joined the Ambulance Service, but Henry had mentored and trained her, and now he believed she was every bit as good as he was, if not better. She was more adaptable to the advances in technology and the frequent changes in policy, while Henry generally preferred the familiar and found it harder and harder to keep up. They were a team, though, complementing each other, with an almost telepathic understanding. They often worked in silence, finding few words were necessary.

Right now, they were checking Nathan Wilde's inert body for vital signs, but they both knew that this young man needed to be made comfortable and transported to hospital as quickly as possible. Even then, it was by no means certain he would make it. The fact Nathan's colleagues were hovering around only made things more difficult. The American was particularly annoying. The blonde was a little calmer, but not greatly, while the other young man just hung about in the background looking terrified.

"You've got to do something!" the American woman insisted.

"Ma'am, we're doing all we can," Henry said, not for the first time. "Now, if we could do our job—"

"You keep saying that, but you're wasting time. He needs to be in hospital now! He's had a stroke, for Christ's sake!"

"Ma'am, I'm aware of his condition. If you could just give us some space to work, we'll be able to get him to the hospital a lot quicker." He nodded to Denise, who gently led Carla Lockhart away.

"We'll do all we can for him," she said, "but you just need to let us get on with it."

"He's only a kid! He shouldn't have had a stroke."

"That's why we need to get him into hospital." Denise turned to Henry. "We good to go, Hen?"

Henry nodded. But before he could move, a shadow appeared on the plastic sheeting behind him and a man stepped through. He looked like he'd been in a fight; he was covered in dust and his face was black in places with dried blood, but he moved with intent and when Henry looked at the man's eyes, they pulsed with a red fire which sent a chill to his core. Henry was a professional, though, and had dealt with many awkward situations. You couldn't be a paramedic in London on a Saturday night without fending off drunks and often potentially violent people.

"I'm sorry, sir, but I'm going to have to ask you to leave this area. We have a very sick man to look after."

Denise joined her partner, providing backup, but could do nothing to prevent the newcomer lashing out a fist, which connected with Henry's head with such force it ended all dreams of retirement cottages in Yorkshire as it sent a shard of skull into Henry's brain, killing him instantly. Denise snatched up her radio to call for assistance, but before she could make the call, the man with the red eyes had grabbed her face with one meaty, filthy hand and, with a twist, snapped her neck. As Denise dropped to the ground, the man turned and looked at Carla, Marianne and Kyle, all three too stunned to move.

"Does anyone else want to join them?" he asked. "No? Good."

He stepped over Denise's corpse and walked over to the workbench where Carla had been examining the exoskeleton.

"I hope you haven't damaged it."

"Now look," Carla said, finally finding her voice, "I don't want any trouble, but you can't just walk in here—"

"Can't?" The man looked around with an exaggerated expression of confusion. Then he grinned. "But I did. I can do whatever I want and you won't stop me. Soon, I will be able to do so much more."

He turned back to the workbench and raised his hands, holding them about a foot above the clay block. As he did so, Carla turned to Marianne and Kyle and hissed, "Get out of here. Now!"

"You come too," Marianne replied.

"Go, stay, do whatever you want," the man said without turning their way. "You can't change anything now."

Marianne looked once more at Carla, then backed out through the plastic sheeting.

Carla Lockhart watched in disbelief as the man's hands began to glow with a red light. The disbelief turned rapidly to horror as pieces of bone tore themselves free of the clay and floated towards the man's arms, ripping through the fabric of his clothing and attaching themselves to his flesh. The glow grew stronger, more intense, and that was the moment when Carla took a fear-frozen Kyle by the arm and dragged him out through the sheeting screen. She got a few feet down the corridor and looked back. The whole of the plastic screen was glowing blood red and, impossible as it seemed, the silhouette of the man had grown wings and was rising off the ground. Then it flexed the wings, and the world exploded around Carla. She was knocked off her feet by the blast and felt her wrist snap as she landed. Kyle crashed down next to her, his dead eyes gazing into her own. She started screaming.

Chapter Twenty-Three

JOEY AND EMMA nearly collided with Marianne Bond as they rushed out of the toilets. She was running down the corridor as if all hell was behind her, and from the sound of the screaming, it seemed like that was possible.

"We've got to get out of here!" Marianne shouted.

"What's happened?" Joey asked. "Was that a bomb?"

"I don't know. It was…I don't know. It's bad. We've got to get out of here. I think they're all dead. That man—"

"What man?" Joey demanded. "Marianne, this is important. What man?"

"I don't know. He just turned up. Oh God, he killed them and then—"

"Listen to me. What did he look like? Was he maybe in his fifties? Hair going grey at the sides?"

"No," Marianne replied. "He was bald. Maybe shaved. Younger. We've got to go!"

"It's not him," Joey said to Emma. "Then who…?" He turned back to Marianne. "Get out of here. See if you can get hold of Raj. Tell him not to come here. It isn't safe."

"What about you?"

"We'll follow. Go on."

Marianne looked doubtfully at him but said, "Good luck," and hurried off up the corridor without looking back.

"If it's not him, who is it?" Joey asked, watching Marianne leave. But Emma wasn't listening.

***

The whisper in Emma's head had started just after they heard the blast.

Emma.

At first, she thought it was the after-effects of the explosion on her ears, but then it came again.

Emma.

It was there and it was a voice she knew very well. It was her own voice. It started off far away, so faint she could barely hear it, but then it became louder and more persistent, and the wound in her hand throbbed in time with the voice.

Emma. Emma. EMMA.

She was aware of Joey talking to the archaeologist woman, but she could hardly concentrate and couldn't even remember the woman's name.

EMMA. EMMA. EMMA.

Joey was speaking to her now, but she couldn't hear him. His voice was getting fainter and fainter, and then it was gone.

***

"Emma?" Joey asked. "Are you okay?"

Emma stood there, holding one hand in the other, her face contorted with pain.

"What is it, Emma? What's happened to your hand?"

Emma looked up at him then, and there were tears streaming down her face.

"She's gone," she said.

"Who? Marianne? I know. I told her—"

"No! Emma's gone."

"What? What do you mean?"

"Your Emma's gone. I can't hear her. It's just me."

"What do you mean she's gone? Where?" Joey took Emma by the shoulder. "Where has she gone?"

"I don't know! There's just me left."

"I've got her," a voice from behind Joey said. "She's safe for now."

Joey turned, but nothing could have prepared him for the sight that greeted him. Floating in the corridor was something out of a horror film. It stood like a man, but its skeleton was on the outside, the bones grafted into flesh. From its back protruded wings made of bone, not feathers, and its eyes burned with a red flame Joey recognised only too well.

"Saunders," he said.

"That's no way to greet an old friend. Not if you want *your* little friend back."

"What have you done with her?" Joey demanded. "If you've hurt her—"

"Joey, look at me. Do you really think you can threaten me? I mean, seriously?" He laughed. "She's safe for now."

"Prove it," Joey said.

"You lost her body, didn't you? When you got here, you'd lost her body. I know where it is, Joey and I can reunite her mind with her body. But time is short. Already her organs are deteriorating. Soon it won't be possible at all."

"Then do it. Please!"

"Only if you do something for me. If you want your girlfriend back, *give me the book*!"

Chapter Twenty-Four

When Liza stopped the car down the road from Charing Cross station, she and Raj were both surprised there were so few people around. They had rehearsed with Anna their reasons for being there—that Anna had spotted them on the street and arrested them—but it looked like it might not be necessary. The area, usually bustling with security personnel, was virtually deserted.

"I don't know that I like this," Raj observed. "Where is everybody?"

"Hang on," Liza replied. "Check *that* out."

As they watched, a black Mercedes pulled up outside the station.

"Government registration plates," Raj said. "It's someone important."

All the same, he was surprised by how important the occupants of the car were. He looked on in astonishment as the doors opened, and first the head of the investigation into the Trafalgar Square blast, and then another figure who was perhaps even more familiar from frequent appearances on the news climbed out.

"Isn't that—what's her name—Frances McCausland?" Liza asked.

"It certainly looks like it," Raj said. "What's the Home Secretary doing here? And why haven't they got minders? They won't have driven themselves here."

"What do we do?"

"Wait and watch. Even with the cover story, we certainly can't get out while they're standing there."

Ducking down as far as they could in their seats, they watched as Martin Buxton and his superior talked for a while. Buxton took a phone call and they talked some more. Then the windows in the station lit up red and, with a sound like a sonic boom, most exploded outwards. Fragments of glass hit the pavement like hailstones, some reaching far enough to bounce off the bonnet of the SUV. Silence followed.

"What the hell was that?" Anna shouted from the back seat.

"No idea." Raj unbuckled his seat belt. "But I think I need to go and find out."

"You can't go in there!" Liza said. "Are you insane? A bomb's just gone off or something. The place is going to be crawling with police and God knows what else any minute. It's probably not safe either."

"McCausland and Buxton have gone in. Look."

"Then they're idiots. Doesn't mean you have to be."

"I think I do. Come if you want or stay here. It's up to you."

Liza sighed heavily. "Someone's got to watch your back."

"Okay, but let's move. Anna, give me the gun."

Anna passed the gun over, but said, "I'm coming too."

"That's not necessary. You stay here and keep your head down. Look after Misha."

"No, Raj. If something's happened, they might need me."

"Fine. Grab Misha's lead and let's go."

"Raj," Liza said. "The kids. You can't leave them here. Someone will have to stay with them."

"We're coming," Evan said.

"You can't just leave us," Ruby pleaded.

"This is ridiculous. They're children, Raj. I can't let you take them in there."

Raj was undecided for a moment, but then turned to the children. "I'd rather you stayed here, but if you're coming, you stick with me. If I tell you to hide, you do it. Is that clear?"

The children nodded enthusiastically.

"I don't believe this," Liza said. "You've lost it big time, Raj."

"It's better if they're with us. At least we can keep an eye on them."

As they got out of the car, the sound of sirens wailed up the street, getting closer.

"Right," Raj said, "stick together and stick close. Let's go and see what's going down."

***

Martin Buxton couldn't believe what he was hearing when, straight after the blast, the Home Secretary told him they had to go inside. He tried to argue, but she had already gone through the station entrance before he could get the words out. All he could do was trail behind, protesting as best he could.

"Home Secretary, really, you shouldn't be here. It isn't safe! There could be another blast!"

The Home Secretary ignored him and strode along, her heels clacking on the concrete floor. She turned down a corridor, and when he followed, he was greeted by a sight which convinced him he had finally gone completely insane. There was something man-shaped but covered in fragments of bone and hovering several feet above the floor. Sprouting from between its shoulder blades were what looked like the skeletal wings of a giant dead bird. In front of the man, or whatever it was, was a teenage boy, who was arguing with it, and a purple-haired girl of about the same age, who was standing to one side with her head in her hands.

Buxton stopped where he was and found he didn't know what to say or how to think. When the Home Secretary went and knelt before this man-thing, Buxton didn't even question it. Nothing made sense anymore, so everything did. He barely even noticed the pain which stabbed at his chest or the fact that breathing had suddenly become harder.

The Home Secretary bowed her head and said, "Master." The winged man turned his head and looked at her with eyes like hot coals.

"You have done well," he said. "I will remember. You may rid yourself of this ridiculous glamour and go now. If I need you again, I will call. I am very grateful to you."

Buxton watched in disbelief as the air around the Home Secretary shimmered and she began to change into something bestial and reptilian. He didn't see the end of this transformation, as the pain slammed into his chest and his left arm and his legs buckled from under him. As he dropped onto his backside on the ground, he had time to think *this is probably just as well* and then he knew nothing.

***

As Raj reached the turn in the corridor, he heard the sound of voices and stopped. He raised a hand and mouthed *stay here.* Liza made a move to go with him, but he placed a hand on her shoulder and shook his head. Then he cocked the gun, pressed his back against the wall and peered around the corner.

There was a great deal to take in at once; something that looked a bit like what Saunders had become at Pendle, only bonier and with wings; Buxton lying on the floor; no sign of the Home Secretary; Emma Winrush cowering to one side, and Joey Cale fronting up to the thing with wings and yelling, "Give her back, Saunders!"

"You know what you have to do," the demon-thing said and raised a hand towards Joey. That was enough for Raj. He rounded the corner, took up a stance and, breathing in, raised the gun. He got in three perfect headshots and then allowed himself to breathe out. The Saunders-demon made a high-pitched rattling gasp and fell face-forward onto the floor. For a second, there was no sound, and then Joey turned on Raj with a fury he had never seen before.

"Raj, you idiot! What the hell did you do that for?"

"Good to see you too, Joey, and yeah, you're welcome."

"He's got Emma. I need him to give her back!"

Raj pointed to the girl who was still standing nearby, terror on her face.

"Isn't that—"

"*My* Emma. The Emma from my...our world. Is Anna with you?"

"Yes, but—"

"She's got to save him, Raj. We can't let him die! He's got to bring Emma back!"

Chapter Twenty-Five

RAJ LOWERED HIS gun and for a while said nothing. He took in the imploring look on his friend's face and then the thing lying on the floor, still twitching occasionally, blood pooling around its head.

Then, and it broke his heart to do so, he said, "No. Sorry, Joey." He went to turn away, but Joey grabbed his jacket and spun him back.

"Don't walk away from me. Is Anna here?"

"Leave it, Joey. I'm sorry about Emma, but I can't let you save him."

"Get out of my way, Raj."

Joey went to side-step past him, but Raj moved to block his path. Joey tried to shove him, but Raj stood fast.

"What's the matter with you?" Joey yelled. "You're a doctor! You're supposed to save lives!"

"What about all the lives he ended when he landed here, Joey? What about them? You can't let him live. Who else is he going to kill? Emma's gone, mate. I'm sorry, but she died at Pendle. You saw it happen."

"She *hasn't* gone!" Joey was nearly weeping with rage now. "She was there, in *her* head. I talked to her. Please, Raj."

"She was."

Joey and Raj both turned as the other Emma found her voice.

"She was in my head, but she's gone. That thing was in my head too, Joey, and it's evil. Don't bring it back."

"It's all right for you," Joey snapped. "You get to live. You can go home if you want. Go on, go back to your life. Forget about all this. Emma can't, can she? She's out there somewhere, and she can't go home!"

Raj had now been joined by the others—Anna, Liza, Evan and Ruby.

"Anna," Joey pleaded. "Help me."

"No, Joey. I don't think so. Raj is right. It has to end here."

"Please. Doesn't Emma deserve a chance?"

"Not if it means doing a deal with him."

"Emma saved us all back at Pendle. All of us! Doesn't that count for anything? Please, Anna. I'm not asking for me. I'm asking for her."

Anna looked first at Joey, then at Raj. "All right. For Emma."

"No, Anna!" Raj protested. "You can't do that. I can't let you!"

"We're healers, Raj. We have to try. Let's get Emma back, and if he's lying about that, I'll put a bullet in his head myself."

She knelt by Saunders' inert body and placed her hands over the three neat holes in the centre of the sections of skull which had fused to his head like a helmet. Raj's shooting had been supremely accurate.

There was a hush as Anna concentrated, which seemed to stretch for hours but was really only minutes. Eventually, she let out a deep sigh. She turned to Joey and shook her head.

"I'm sorry. There's nothing. I don't even know what I'm dealing with here. Maybe it only works on us."

Joey took a slow breath and looked down at the winged body on the floor.

"Okay," he said, finally. "You tried, Anna. Thank you. You win, Raj."

"Good man," Raj said. "Come on. We need to get out of here."

"You go on. I just need a minute to say goodbye."

"To him?"

"To Emma."

"Fine. But don't be long. There are going to be police all over the place and I'm not sure how long Anna can convince them she's their boss."

"I won't be a minute. Go on." Joey turned to the Emma of this world. "Go home to your mum. Look after her."

She gave him a weak smile and went to join Raj and the others. Silently, they all walked away, only Raj looking back.

***

Joey waited until their footsteps receded and said, "They're gone."

At first, there was no response, but then there came the sound of bone scraping against stone, and Saunders slowly clambered first to his knees and then to his feet. He wiped away some of the blood which had congealed on the side of his face and laughed.

"That was very well done, Joey. You're quite the actor. You nearly even convinced me. That went better than we thought. I didn't expect your friend to shoot me, though. At least Anna sorted the headache out, among other things.

"I've done my bit," Joey said. "Now give Emma back."

"Just a minute."

Saunders closed his eyes. Outside, the wail of sirens abruptly changed pitch like a record played on the wrong speed.

"That's better. I've slowed your police down a bit. We don't want any interruptions, because we haven't quite finished here. There is one thing you still have to do. The book? Go and get it. And I suggest you don't try anything. Emma will be very glad to see you again."

Joey hesitated, but Saunders opened his arms wide and when he spoke again, his voice was calm and reasonable.

"Think about it, Joey. I have gone to a great deal of trouble for this moment. Through my agent, I have taken over the Government of this country, just so everyone would be in the right place at the right time. Why do you think I arranged for Emma to be arrested when you first met her? I wanted her kept safe for you. I couldn't risk anything happening to her before I was ready. I have done all this to reunite her body and her mind, and I have done it for you. All I am asking is one little thing in return. It's not too much to ask, is it?"

Joey was still thinking about it. Saunders raised a bone-encrusted eyebrow and smiled.

"Wait there," Joey said.

"Oh, don't worry. I'm not going anywhere. I have all the time in the world."

Joey hurried along the corridor to the toilets and pushed open the door. The book was still where it had fallen under the sink. He snatched it up and rushed back to where Saunders was waiting. When he saw him returning, Saunders held out his hand, but Joey hesitated.

"Emma," he said.

"If you give me the book, I'll be complete, now that Anna's tender ministrations have helped this pathetic body bond to my—shall we say—remains? I'll be able to take you to Emma and then send you both home. You'll see your parents again. You want that, don't you?"

"I don't trust you."

"I know, and I don't really blame you. But you have to understand, Joey, that no matter what you think, I'm not evil. Good and evil are concepts your lot have invented. They don't mean anything to us—we just *are*. We do what we need to do to exist. If you want to see Emma again, you'll have to trust me. You really don't have a choice. But if you need proof, I can do that. Open your mind and I will show you."

Joey hesitated again, but found his eyes being drawn towards Saunders' own. His mind went black for a second and then a picture started to form. It was hazy at first, but the haze began to clear, and he could see a motionless form lying on a rock, somewhere dark and gloomy. He knew instantly it was Emma—the Emma he had known and come so close to loving. He wanted to reach out and touch her, to be sure she was real.

"Where is she?" he asked, and as soon as he spoke, he was back in the station, looking into Saunders' eyes. He blinked and looked away.

"She's safe, Joey. Give me the book and I will take you there. You can watch while I restore her mind. She will be very pleased to see you."

"If I give you the book, what then? You said you'll be complete, but what will you do?"

"I'll live, Joey. That's all. I'll live."

Joey felt the weight of the book in his hand and badly wanted to throw it away and run, but instead he held it out. Saunders took it and held it to his chest, breathing deeply.

"Thank you," he said. "I've waited a long time to get this back."

"One thing," Joey said. "If you can send me home, can you send the others home too? Raj and Anna and the kids?"

"I can do that. Even the dog."

"Then do it," Joey said. "I'm ready."

He closed his eyes and concentrated on his heart, feeling it slow, then stop. There was a sensation of the world shifting around him. Then he felt nothing.

***

Emma Winrush was walking alone next to this group of strangers who all seemed to know each other but were largely ignoring her. Only the two peculiar children kept looking at her as if she was supposed to know who they were, but she had no idea what to say to them. Their faces were somewhere in her head but it was like a distant memory. She just wanted to go home and put all this behind her. But because the children kept looking her way, she was the one who saw them disappear. One second, they were walking along in front of her, the next, they had vanished like smoke.

"Er, excuse me?" Emma said. "The kids—"

The man called Raj turned around, irritation showing in his face.

"Come on, Evan. We haven't got time for this."

"Ruby's gone, too, Raj," the woman—Anna—said. "She can't do that trick—" Before she could say any more, she had vanished too.

"Anna?" Raj called. He quickly turned to the woman by his side. "Carry on, Liza," he said. "Whatever happens, carry—" But the sentence never got finished because it was if Raj and Misha had never been there.

"Thanks, Raj," Liza muttered. "You always did leave me to clear up your bloody messes.

She turned to Emma and smiled, but Emma saw the tears welling in her eyes.

Liza wiped her face on her sleeve. "Come on," she said. "Let's see if we can get you home."

Epilogue

BLACK BECAME RED and then…light.

Joey opened his eyes a crack, and the light flooded in. It hurt, so he closed his eyes again.

"Joey?" The voice came from somewhere nearby, and he tried opening his eyes again, more slowly this time. The light was dazzling, but he could make out the shape of a person in front of him.

"Joey? Can you hear me? My name's Anna."

Of course it is, Joey thought and went back to sleep.

When he woke up again, he found he could open his eyes without pain. His head was resting on something soft, but there was something down his throat and he couldn't move his arms. His first instinct was to panic, but a voice from somewhere out of sight soothed.

"Joey, it's okay. You're safe now. You're in hospital. Try and rest and I'll get the doctor."

Joey stopped struggling and tried to rest. *Hospital.* That was good.

The next time he woke up, he was aware of someone leaning over him. It was a man dressed in blue scrubs, and he seemed familiar somehow.

"Hello, Joey," he said. "Welcome back. You've been through a bit of a time of it, I'm afraid, but you're safe now. My name is Doctor Chowdhury. You're in hospital. Do you remember what happened to you?"

Joey found he couldn't speak because of whatever it was that was down his throat, so he shook his head instead.

"You were in an accident—quite a serious one. You walked out in front of a car and it hit you. Don't you remember?"

Joey shook his head again. There was something at the back of his mind about a car, but he couldn't bring it into focus. *A silver car?* He couldn't be sure.

"You were knocked unconscious, and you've been out for nearly two weeks now. Everyone's been worried about you, but it looks like you're going to be okay. The consultant will be round to see you soon, but I don't think it will be long before we can get that tube out of your throat. In the meantime, keep resting."

Joey began to drift off again. He still sort of remembered a car but couldn't remember the accident.

He slept for another three hours. When he woke up again, there was a different man standing over the bed, an older man with dark hair going grey at the sides.

"Hello, Joey," he said with a smile. "I'm Mr. Saunders. You've been in the wars, haven't you? Well, don't worry. You're exactly where you need to be now."

TO BE CONCLUDED

Praise For *Missing Beat*

"*Missing Beat* is a page turner. I ploughed through the first 22 chapters before I had to take a break. Stone ends chapters, spring-boarding us in another direction or with hands clutched to mouth. He also creates a new, unique world and it is terrifying, not only because of the Screamers but also because it is so much like our own world but with chilling differences."

Ruth Estevez
Author – *Jiddy Vardy*

"A sure sign of a great story is reading the whole lot in one go – and the minute I met Joey Cale I had to stay with him to find out what happens next. An intriguing premise, with characters to care about – it is very much a page-turner. Eagerly awaiting the next book now."

Elaine Wickson
Author – *Planet Stan*

"I would recommend this book to adults both young and older. I think I read it in two sittings, just could not put it down. I will not spoil the surprise by giving any details away, suffice to say if you read it, like myself, you will be looking forward to the next in the trilogy."

Zack – aged 14

"*Missing Beat* is one of those books you get so engrossed in you forget…to eat. (And for me, there is no higher praise.) Bob Stone has taken the idea of 'disability' and turned it on its head. In Joey, he has a main protagonist who you'd really like to be; he is kind and considerate, with totally uncheesy charm. It immediately makes you care about him as he faces real dangers in an intriguing other world. The other characters are well drawn, with believably distinct and natural dialogue… This is a cracking first novel."

Suzie Wilde
Author – *The Book of Bera, Obsidian*

"Awesome book. Read it in one sitting. Gripping from start to finish."

Jon Mayhew
Author – *Mortlock, The Demon Collector*

"So many twists and turns, a plot both complex and astonishing – and then BOOM, cliffhanger to end all cliffhangers – well done!"

Kathryn Evans
Author – *More of Me, Beauty Sleep*

"If you love inter-dimensional mysteries with real characters rather than superheroes, you'll love this like I did"

Paul Magrs
Author – *Doctor Who, Heart of Mars*

Acknowledgements

Your second book is harder than your first book. Ask anyone. They will pretty much all say the same. The fact that there is a second book at all is down to the faith of an embarrassingly large number of people, too numerous to name individually. But if you're reading this because you read and enjoyed *Missing Beat*, then consider yourself named. If you read it, enjoyed it *and* reviewed it, consider yourself at the top table of those named. Thank you all. Really. Without you, I would never have started writing *Beat Surrender*, let alone be writing an acknowledgements page to finish it off.

There are a few individuals I must single out, though. Tim Quinn interviewed me at the launch of *Missing Beat* and gave me such an incredible build-up I wanted to sit back down and make way for this awesome person he was talking about. I have long admired Tim's work and it meant the world.

Then there is Debbie McGowan and, in fact, the whole family at Beaten Track Publishing. Debbie is the best publisher, editor and friend you could wish for. She makes you want to be better, and there are times when we all need that. My books would not be possible without her. The rest of the Beaten Track family of authors, editors and proofreaders are always there to pick you up when you are down and encourage you to go on.

If you looked at the cover of this book and thought, as I did, "Wow! That's another corker!", that's because the mega-talented Trevor Howarth designed it, so what did you expect?

Finally, I cannot conclude these acknowledgements without thanking Wendy. She is my reason for all things and without her, there is no me. Love you always.

About the Author

Liverpool born Bob Stone is an author and bookshop owner. He has been writing for as long as he could hold a pen and some would say his handwriting has never improved. He is the author of two self-published children's books, *A Bushy Tale* and *A Bushy Tale: The Brush Off*. *Missing Beat*, the first in a trilogy for Young Adults, was his first full-length novel.

Bob still lives in Liverpool with his wife and cat and sees no reason to change any of that.

By the Author

A Bushy Tale

A Bushy Tale: The Brush Off

Missing Beat

Out of Season

Beat Surrender

Beaten Track Publishing

For more titles from Beaten Track Publishing,
please visit our website:

https://www.beatentrackpublishing.com

Thanks for reading!

Lightning Source UK Ltd.
Milton Keynes UK
UKHW040608140319
339119UK00001B/2/P